SCARY STORIES
for Sleep-Overs

SCARY STORIES
for Sleep-Overs

By R. C. Welch
Illustrated by Ricardo Delgado

An RGA Book

PRICE STERN SLOAN
Los Angeles

Copyright © 1991 RGA Publishing Group, Inc.
Illustrations copyright © RGA Publishing Group, Inc.,
and Richard Delgado.
Published by Price Stern Sloan, Inc.,
A member of The Putnam & Grosset Group,
New York, New York.

9 11 13 14 12 10 8
ISBN: 0-8431-2914-X

Library of Congress Cataloging-in-Publication Data

Welch, Robert, 1962-
    Scary stories for sleep-overs / by Robert Welch.
        p.   cm.
    Summary: A collection of scary short stories.
    ISBN 0-8431-2914-X
    1. Horror tales, American. 2. Children's stories, American.
[1. Horror stories. 2. Short stories.] I. Title.
PZ7.W44888Sc 1991
[Fic]—dc20   91-18587
                                                        CIP
                                                        AC

Designed by Michele Lanci-Altomare

To Lary Gibson, who shaped the flame,
and Tatiana, who fuels it
—R. C. W.

To my wife Frances, the best thing in my life
—R. D.

Contents

SCARY STORIES
for Sleep-Overs

The Hermit of Collins Peak

Rickie and his friends were telling Kurt, the new boy in the neighborhood, about the strange old hermit who lived outside of town.

"He's crazy," Rickie was saying. The other boys nodded. "He lives in a shack over on Collins Peak."

"A shack?" Kurt asked.

"I swear!" said Rickie, holding up his hand.

"It's true," added Steve, Rickie's best friend. "He built it against the side of the mountain with old pieces of metal and wood."

Kurt shook his head. "That's really weird. Who is this guy?"

Some of the boys shrugged. "His name is Collins," said Sean. "He's lived up there forever—as long as anybody can remember. That's why they call it Collins Peak."

"My grandma told me once that he had a sad story," said Nathan. "But that's all she'd say."

"It's a sad story, all right," agreed Rickie. "He's a crazy old man who lives in a shack!" The rest of the boys laughed.

"What does he do up there?" asked Kurt.

"Nothing," replied Rickie. "He never talks to anyone. He never comes into town."

"We think he eats kids," said Steve.

"What?" Kurt asked.

"It's true," said Rickie. "He hates kids. Everyone at school knows it. His shack's at the end of a big field, and anytime somebody sets foot on it, he comes screaming out of nowhere."

"Get outta here!" yelled Sean in his deepest voice. He pulled his head down between his shoulders and limped around in a circle. "You stupid kids! Get outta here and leave me alone!"

"If I catch you I'll turn your backsides red!" Steve added. Everyone laughed at that.

"Yeah," continued Rickie. "Sometimes we dare each other to see who can get the closest to his shack before he comes charging out."

"Why do you say he *eats* kids?" asked Kurt.

"Well," said Rickie, his voice dropping lower as he leaned toward Kurt, "you never know where he is. He sneaks all over these hills, waiting for some kid to do something stupid, like wander in alone. Then it's all over."

"Wh—what happens?" Kurt asked.

"He'll trap that kid. Take him back to his shack, where he cooks him slowly over a fire. Then he stores the blackened body carefully so it'll last him for his next few meals. There's a pit nearby that's filled with the rotten bones of every kid who's ever disappeared around here."

Kurt looked at Rickie suspiciously. "And how many kids is that?"

Rickie shrugged. "Don't know. But you'd better be careful, or you'll be one of them."

At that moment, Sean grabbed Kurt from behind and yelled, "Gotcha!" Kurt squealed and jumped, and the rest of the boys howled with laughter.

"Rotten bones. Yeah, right!" Kurt smiled and shook his head. "Okay. You got me."

After the boys recovered, Nathan said, "Who knows why he really doesn't like us to get near his stupid shack. Maybe he's got some kind of treasure hidden there. Why else would he care about anyone coming around? Heck, he's been living in those hills for ages. Who knows what he's found. Maybe he's found some kind of gold mine!"

"Then why doesn't he spend a lot of money?" demanded Sean.

"Maybe because then he knows people would come up there and kick him out," guessed Steve.

"Maybe he had a partner and killed him to keep the gold for himself," Kurt suggested. They spent the rest of the afternoon making up wild stories about the old man.

That night, Kurt asked his parents if they had heard about the hermit. His father shook his head, but his mother nodded that she had heard something once.

"Mrs. Beecham was telling me about him," she explained. "He used to live in town a long time ago. His wife died giving birth to his only son. Then, a few years later, his son disappeared. Apparently he went a little crazy after that. He built some kind of house up on Collins Peak, and he's lived there ever since."

"I hadn't heard that," Kurt's father said. "Is he supposed to be dangerous?"

"Mrs. Beecham didn't think so. She said he's lived there longer than most of the people have in this town. He's never hurt anybody."

"Rickie was telling me that he hates kids and chases them away whenever they come near his shack," said Kurt.

His father laughed. "I can see it now. Some poor old guy living up in the hills. He must be a target for every kid within a hundred miles!" He turned to Kurt. "I'm sure Rickie is right. This guy has probably been pestered by kids ever since he moved up there. Why don't you just leave him in peace, okay?"

Kurt shrugged. "Sure, Dad." He bent over his plate and paid close attention to his dinner.

The next day he couldn't wait to talk to his new friends. They all met at Steve's house, and Kurt filled them in on what his mother had told him.

"See?" said Rickie. "That just proves it! He probably hates kids because he lost his son!"

"Let's show Kurt the shack," suggested Sean.

"I don't know," Kurt said. "My dad said I should leave the old man alone. I think he feels sorry for him."

"Don't worry," said Rickie. "We'll just go as far as the edge of the field. Then you can see what we're talking about."

Kurt pretended to resist, but was soon heading out of town to Collins Peak with the rest of the boys. They walked to the end of Adler Road, which turned into a dirt trail winding its way into the foothills. Rickie led them to a point where the trail began to bend around the mountain.

"Just up around that bend," he said to Kurt in a low voice, "is the old man's field. When we get there, look toward the far end and you'll see his shack."

They crept along the trail and gradually a field was revealed. It lay to the right of the trail and was surrounded on three sides by steep slopes. It was about as big as a football field, and at the far end stood the hermit's shack.

To Kurt, it looked as if the shack were crouched under the oak trees, waiting to pounce on an unsuspecting child. He had no idea how it was held together. There were all different kinds and sizes of metal sheets, aluminum siding, wooden planks and pieces of plastic. It hunched up against the side of the mountain, as if any minute it would push against the hill so as to lunge forward all the better.

"He lives *there*?" Kurt asked in disbelief.

"That's right," said Rickie. "Nice place, huh?"

Suddenly the door of the shack swung open, and the old man rushed out. Kurt figured he must be more than a hundred years old! His body was thin, and his bones poked through the holes in his ragged clothes. He had long, white hair that stuck straight out and a scraggly beard that hung down to his chest.

He looked anxiously around the clearing. The boys shrunk back into the bushes, peeking through the branches. Kurt felt as if the old man were looking straight at him! But nothing happened. The hermit began coughing, and even from where they were, Kurt could hear the horrible gasping. Then the old man ducked back into his hut.

Rickie motioned to the others, and they backed away down the trail. Once out of sight of the field, they ran all the way back to Adler Road. Then they stumbled to a halt, chests heaving.

"See?" said Nathan. "He is one strange-looking old man!"

"It sounded like he was about to die!" said Rickie.

The boys started walking again. They spent the rest of the day playing hide-and-seek in the overgrown weeds and bushes near the end of Adler Road.

One morning a few weeks later, Kurt was eating his breakfast when the doorbell rang. "I got it," he yelled, and ran to the front door. It was Sean.

"Kurt! Get dressed!"

"Why? What's up?" Kurt let Sean in and they went to his room.

"Guess what happened last night when Mr. Grafton was walking his dog?"

"How should I know?" Kurt was lacing up his shoes. "What's going on?"

"Mr. Grafton was walking that goofy German shepherd of his up around Adler Road when the dog starts going crazy. So Grafton lets the dog go, and it runs over to some bushes and starts barking."

"Yeah?" Kurt prompted. He forgot about tying his other shoe. "What was it?"

"The old man! He had some kind of heart attack or something! So Grafton got the police and an ambulance up there, and they took the old man to the hospital!"

"Wow! How do you know all this?" asked Kurt.

Sean practically did a dance. "My sister works at the hospital. She told us at breakfast this morning."

"Is he dead?"

"Nah. But do you know what this means?"

"What?"

"It means," said Sean, becoming very serious, "that for the first time since I can remember, the old man is *not* at his shack!"

Kurt realized what Sean was suggesting and started to protest.

"Come on!" Sean cut in. "Rickie, Steve and Nathan are going to meet us at Adler Road!"

Kurt stood up, chewing on his lip while he thought. Sean watched. Then Kurt grinned and threw his arms in the air like a champion boxer. "Yes!" he yelled. "Let's go!"

· · · · · · · · · ·

The old man was dying, and he knew it. He opened his eyes and stared at the white walls of the hospital room. He hadn't been in a hospital since his son was born. He turned slowly and looked at the tube in his arm, smiling bitterly. There was no use, but try and tell that to a doctor.

Yes, he knew he was dying. He had known it since the coughing began, nearly six months ago. First he thought he had a slight cold, or maybe bronchitis at the worst. But the cough never went away. After the first couple of weeks, it felt like his chest was being ripped apart every time he coughed. And not long after that, he had started coughing up blood.

He felt himself falling asleep again. He was so tired. Then he remembered. The cave! He had to tell someone about the cave! He struggled into a sitting position and reached for the nurse's bell.

· · · · · · · · · ·

Rickie, Nathan and Steve were already at the end of Adler Road by the time Sean and Kurt got there. Rickie showed the others his Swiss army knife.

"What's that for?" asked Kurt.

"Be prepared," intoned Rickie. "That's the scout motto."

Steve rolled his eyes. "Great. We'll call you if we need a fish scaled. Let's get going."

They started up the road. Soon they got to the trail that led up the foothills and to the old man's shack. With mounting excitement, they continued.

· · · · · · · · · ·

The nurse ran into the room. "Mr. Collins!" she said, prying his fingers from the bell. "What's the matter?"

He grabbed at her wrist and tried to talk. But he felt that sharp familiar feeling in his chest and began coughing. Only this time he couldn't seem to stop. He held onto the nurse as his body shook, and flecks of blood sprayed from his mouth.

"Mr. Collins," she said, frightened. "Mr. Collins! Let me get the doctor!"

He shook his head, and with a huge effort he forced himself to stop. "No," he gasped. "Wait! My hut . . . the cave!" He blacked out for a moment, and the nurse hit the intercom and asked for a doctor.

• • • • • • • • • •

The boys reached the field and marched bravely toward the far end. As they got closer to the shack, some of their courage leaked away, and they moved slower.

"What if he's been released?" asked Kurt.

"No way," said Sean. "My sister said they'll have to monitor him for at least twenty-four hours."

"But what if there's someone else in there?" whispered Steve.

They stopped a few feet in front of the shack. "Hello?" called Rickie. "Anybody home?" They waited, their nerves on edge. But all was silent. The one window of the shack was dark and empty.

"Come on," said Rickie suddenly. He strode forward before the others could react and pulled open the door.

They all braced themselves for some kind of howling demon to rush out and devour Rickie, but nothing happened. The other boys edged closer.

"Hey!" said Rickie. "Look at that!"

Kurt couldn't believe it. The back wall of the shack had a door in it. Yet the back wall was up against the hillside.

"You see," said Nathan proudly. "I was right! He did find a gold mine!"

The rest of the hut was quickly examined and judged worthless. There was nothing in it but an old chest of drawers with some scraps of clothing, a small table and a bed. A bowl with some shriveled fruit in it sat on the table.

Rickie positioned himself in front of the back door. It had a bar across it that could easily be lifted off. He looked at the other boys. "Ready, men?"

• • • • • • • • • •

Old man Collins swung his mind out of the blackness. The nurse was there, explaining to the doctor why she had called him. The doctor leaned over him.

"Mr. Collins," he said gently. "You're in pretty bad shape."

"Doesn't matter," he gasped. "My hut—"

"Your hut will be fine," the doctor tried to calm him. "Now please try to relax."

Mr. Collins grabbed at the doctor's arm, but his strength failed him. He began coughing again. This time, he felt something tear in his chest, and after a sharp pain there was nothing. His vision grew dimmer, and his hand slipped from the doctor's arm.

He was no longer in the hospital room. Instead, he floated over the field where his hut stood. Then he was inside the hut, watching as the boys approached the back door.

"No!" he yelled. "Get away from there!" But they couldn't hear him.

"Ready, men?" he heard one of the boys say. The boy grabbed the bar across the back door.

"Stay away!" the old man yelled again. "I'm trying to protect you! Get outta there!" It was no use.

The boy slid the bar to the side, and threw open the door. Behind the door was the dark mouth of a cave. As one, the boys pushed forward to peer inside. Then each of them felt an invisible force grab at them with terrible strength and pull them deeper inside the cave.

"No!" screamed Mr. Collins with all his might. It was the last thing he ever said.

• • • • • • • • • •

"What was he yelling about, Doctor?" the nurse asked as she looked down at the dead body of Mr. Collins.

"Delirium," answered the doctor. "Who knows what they see just before they go."

Dead Giveaway

erry woke up and looked at the clock. "Oh no," he groaned. Time to get up already. Then he remembered. There was no school today! He lay back on his pillow and tried to figure out how he should feel about classes being canceled. There were no classes because of Mrs. Stowe's funeral. She had been the fifth grade teacher, Terry's teacher. A couple of days ago she had died in a car crash.

Terry stared at the ceiling. His ex-teacher had always seemed to pick on him, and they had developed a mutual dislike for each other over the year. In fact, the day she died, the same day Midnight had run away, he had been so mad at her he had wished something would happen to her. She had embarrassed him in front of the whole class. When she found out he hadn't done the homework assignment, she made him come up to the blackboard while she instructed him to write the assignment—as if he were a second-grader!

When he had heard that something had happened to Mrs. Stowe, he felt guilty. He had never wished she would be killed, that was for sure!

Suddenly, a black object leaped through the open window and landed on Terry's stomach. "Hey!" he yelled. "Midnight, you're back!"

The green-eyed cat looked up at Terry from her landing pad and began purring. She had found Terry nearly a week ago. He had been walking home from school when out of nowhere Midnight had appeared. She ran right up to him and started rubbing against his leg. He examined her and she looked pretty healthy, but there was no identifying collar. He played with her for a bit, and when he came home, she followed him. He had named her Midnight because her fur was the deepest, darkest black he had ever seen. Then, just when the whole family was getting used to her, she ran away. Boy, Terry was glad to have her back!

His mother came into the room. "Well, look who's back!" she said, walking towards Midnight to pet her. But the cat completely ignored her and nuzzled Terry's side. "Well, I guess she only has eyes for you!" Then she added, "Don't forget we're going to Mrs. Stowe's funeral today, Terry."

"Come on, Mom. How could I forget that?"

His mother smiled. "You'd find a way."

• • • • • • • • • •

Most of the fifth grade class was at the funeral. Terry made sure to stand by Scott, his best friend.

"This is pretty weird," Scott whispered halfway through the ceremony. "I mean, one day she's here making us do loads of homework, and the next day—poof!"

Terry nodded. "I know," he whispered back. "It's not like she was my favorite teacher or anything, but geez!"

"I heard she died instantly. An eyewitness said he saw a dark object run in front of the car."

"Who told you that?" Terry demanded.

Terry's mother hushed him before he got his answer, and he turned forward. The minister gave a long speech about Mrs. Stowe's dedication to her students. He was followed by Mr. Keller, the school principal. Terry tried not to fidget. But he really wanted to know more about what Scott had said.

After the funeral, the kids piled back into their parents' cars. Terry talked his mom into letting him and Scott walk back to the house together.

"What did you mean when you said a dark object ran in front of Mrs. Stowe's car?" Terry asked as soon as his mother was out of earshot.

"Ryan heard his dad talking about it. He said she swerved to miss it and ran right into a tree—BOOM!"

It was possible, Terry thought. After all, Ryan's dad was a policeman. "Do they have any idea what this dark object was?"

"Ryan says they don't have a clue. It was really hauling."

They reached Terry's house, and spent the rest of the morning reading comic books. Scott had to go home at lunchtime to watch his little brother. Terry flipped on the television and sat on the couch. Soon, Midnight came into the room and curled up against his leg.

He wondered about Mrs. Stowe and shivered. No matter how stupid she made him feel, he could never have wished death on her. No, that kind of punishment had to be reserved for people who really deserved it. Like Howard, the school bully.

Terry grunted. All the kids hated Howard. He was the biggest kid in the sixth grade, and he beat up on everybody. Once he had sent Terry home with a cut lip. And Terry had been too frightened to tell his parents what had really happened. He had told them he'd fallen on the playground.

Yeah, he thought with a nod of his head. *Howard was a person who deserved to be torn to shreds!*

The next day was school as usual. But when Terry got there the playground was buzzing with excitement. Scott ran over to him as soon as he saw him.

"You're not going to believe this, Terry!" Scott practically yelled. He had a wild look, and his voice sounded shaky. "Howard fell into the lion's den at the zoo and was torn to shreds!"

"He . . . he's dead?" Terry stammered.

"Yeah, they're saying something scared him and he fell in!"

Terry felt a chill creep over his skin, as if some unseen hand were plucking at his arm hairs. "Howard?" he asked in a low voice. "Are you serious?"

Scott nodded like his head would fall off. "I know! I know! I didn't believe it either. But he didn't show up for class this morning. And then Mr. Keller came by and made the announcement that Howard had been found dead!"

Terry listened all day to everyone buzzing about Howard's death, and as the day wore on, he found himself beginning to panic. *Could it be?*

He had trouble concentrating during class and was almost surprised when the bell rang at the end of the day. He caught a ride home with Scott and his mother, and when he got there he practically ran inside. He slammed the door behind himself and dove onto the couch.

Was it possible—? No! It couldn't be! He buried his head in his hands and tried to convince himself he had nothing to do with Howard's or Mrs. Stowe's death.

His mind was racing. He couldn't help thinking about a television movie he once saw—about a man who had trouble with his memory. And at the end of the movie, the man found out that during his blackouts he had been murdering people. "Is that what's happening to me?" Terry wondered out loud.

No, that was impossible. Mrs. Stowe died in a car crash. And as for Howard . . . sure, he had just been thinking that it was Howard's turn for some punishment. But there was no way that he could have had anything to do with that— Howard had had an accident at the zoo.

It had to be a coincidence, Terry finally convinced himself. He felt a little better after that, and went to his room to do some homework.

The rest of the month passed uneventfully. Terry's mother left town to help out her sister, who was in the hospital. Terry slowly forgot about his suspicions that he was a deranged killer who unconsciously murdered everybody he didn't like. Instead, he started to think about his friend Diane's birthday party at the end of the month. The entire fifth grade class was going, and it was shaping up to be the event of the semester.

The Friday before the party, everyone was making plans to meet the next day. Terry got home and did all his homework so he wouldn't have to worry about it over the weekend. Then, because his dad still hadn't come home, he made himself a sandwich to snack on. Midnight came strolling in, and Terry chased her around the kitchen. Then she darted into the living room and began racing around with Terry in hot pursuit. Suddenly, she tore down the hall, and when Terry jumped after her he crashed against the corner of his dad's display case. He yelled and stumbled to the floor, then his blood chilled as he heard the sound of breaking glass.

He slowly turned to look. The display case stood on four thin legs, and had two glass doors. Inside was his father's collection of old camera equipment. Now the case lay toppled over, and Terry knew with a sick feeling what he would find when he stood it up.

Sure enough, the glass doors had broken when the ancient projector had fallen against them. What Terry didn't know was whether or not he had ruined the cameras and projector as well. He cleaned up the mess as best as he could, and waited in agony until his father came home.

His father noticed the damage the minute he walked in. "What happened here?" he asked in a disturbingly quiet voice.

"I'm sorry, Dad. I was chasing Midnight and I tripped and fell against the case. It was an accident!"

His father didn't say anything right away, but walked over to inspect his collection. Then he turned to Terry. "You know better than that."

Terry hung his head. That was the worst part—he did know he wasn't supposed to run around the living room. "Yes," he admitted.

His father nodded. "Yes, you do." He studied the shattered glass doors. "Well, I'm going to have to go and get some glass cut tomorrow. Then I'll see if I can re-hang those doors. And I think while I'm out, that would be a perfect time for you to sit quietly and think about why I make rules about what you should and should not be doing in the house."

With dawning horror, Terry realized what his father was saying. "You mean, I'm grounded?" he asked in panic.

"That's exactly what I mean."

"But Dad! You can't . . . not tomorrow! Diane's party is tomorrow! Everybody will be there!"

"Not everybody. Because you'll be here." His father turned to look at him. "No arguments."

Terry opened and closed his mouth silently. He could feel hot tears beginning to burn his eyes. He knew it was useless to argue. He ran to his room and threw himself on the bed.

It wasn't fair! He didn't mean to knock the stupid case down. His tears filled his eyes and ran down his cheeks. Why did his dad have to be so mean?

Midnight came in and jumped on the bed next to him. Terry angrily shoved her away. "Get out of here, you stupid cat! It's all your fault." He started to really cry then.

Later, at dinner, he tried to persuade his father to change his mind. He offered to stay home Sunday instead, or all weekend next week. But his father wouldn't budge. Terry went to bed in a black mood and fell asleep planning to run away. That would teach his father to not be so hateful!

In the middle of the night he heard a loud thud. He opened his eyes and looked around the room. Then he switched on the light at the side of his bed.

Midnight had pushed the door open slightly and was slinking into the room. Terry watched her curiously. Some trick of the light made Midnight seem bigger than usual. Then Terry remembered the thud. He also remembered he had gone to bed very angry at his father.

His father! Maybe that's where the thud came from. Maybe his father was in trouble! He ran out of his room and searched frantically through the house. He couldn't find his father! Just as he was thinking the thud was in his imagination, Terry saw a dim light coming from the basement. He ran to the basement door and found it wide open. He stood at the top of the stairs and looked down, afraid of what he might see.

There, crumpled in a heap at the base of the stairs, was his father. "Dad!" Terry screamed in anguish as he raced down the stairs to his father's lifeless body.

Slowly, as he wept over his father, Terry noticed something rubbing against his leg. Then he heard the purring.

"Midnight!" he shrieked. "It's you!" He tried to grab the dark animal, now almost twice its size, but she leaped out of his reach, purring wildly.

"What *are* you?!" Terry cried, tears streaming down his face. He grabbed a baseball bat from behind the door. Then he swung it at the huge cat.

Midnight jumped aside and Terry missed. He was panting with fear and almost blinded by tears. But he was

still able to see the change coming over the cat.

She was turning into a monster, prowling back and forth, her tail cutting through the air like a whip. And with each turn she took, her body swelled even larger.

Terry threw the bat at the creature and practically flew up the basement stairs. He quickly slammed the door behind him just before the gigantic cat got through.

For a moment he stood there, gasping for breath, trying to figure out what to do. Just as he was getting his mind to accept what was happening, a crashing blow shook the basement door in its frame.

Terry jumped back and watched in terrified fascination as blow after blow hit the door. Then, with a noise like a saw blade cutting through wood, a huge black paw tore through the door. Terry backed slowly away, his mind no longer functioning. He watched the big black cat try to push its way through the hole. It now stood nearly as tall as Terry at its shoulders.

Terry turned to run. There was a roar from behind him and the door splintered apart. He ran into the hall bathroom and slammed the door behind him. A second later, the monster hit it from the other side.

Terry clawed frantically at the bathroom window while the cat battered at the door. Then, with a final thought that snapped his mind, he remembered that the window was barred on the outside. Numbly, he turned to face the bathroom door, just as the cat began to shoulder its way through.

The Gift

ason poked a pencil at the ants. The little black insects exploded into action, running around in tight circles and bumping into each other.

Jason chuckled and scraped the pencil back and forth in the dirt, covering the hole to the ants' nest. The workers scurried around crazily. Jason watched them for a while, then stepped away from his dresser and tossed the pencil back onto his desk. He sat glumly on his bed with his chin in his hands.

Then he heard rapping at his bedroom window and turned around to look.

"Hey!" said Eddie, Jason's neighbor, from outside the

window. "Wanna come down to the fort with me and Mitch?"

"I can't," said Jason with disgust. "I've got to stay inside today."

"Why?"

"I got grounded."

Eddie snorted. "What for?"

Jason waved a hand at the ant farm. "My cousin gave me that for my birthday, and I told him I thought it was a dumb gift." He sighed. "And now my dad's making me stay inside as a 'lesson in politeness.'"

Eddie laughed with the careless freedom of someone who's outside on a warm summer day. He jumped back from the window. "All right. See you later."

Jason watched him run down the street. His eyes were drawn back to the unwanted gift on top of his dresser. He still couldn't figure out why his cousin would give him something like that. He thought it was a pretty stupid gift; a flat, plastic box filled with dirt and a bunch of black ants. If he wanted to watch ants, he could go out in the backyard! There were about a hundred other things he could think of that would have made a better gift.

He stared at the farm on top of his dresser. "I should just throw it away," he mumbled. But he knew his parents would get even more angry if he did that. They might ground him for the rest of the month. He stood up and shook the farm. The ant tunnels collapsed as the dirt shifted around.

"Stupid ants," Jason said and left the room.

He tried watching TV but soon grew bored with that. He

went out in the backyard for a while, but he grew tired of that, too. He could normally spend hours in the garden playing with his gang of superheroes—but not when he was *forced* to.

He trudged back to his room to find something to do. His eyes narrowed as he spied the industrious ants rebuilding their tunnels and nests. He shook the plastic container again, sending the ants scurrying to dig out their trapped comrades.

He decided to fix lunch. While he was searching for the mustard, an idea came to him. Grabbing a bottle of vinegar from the cupboard, he went back to his room and poured a few drops on the ants.

The results were pretty disappointing. The ants didn't like it, of course; but all they really did was scutter away and perform some strange ritual that looked as if they were trying to clean themselves.

Jason tried a lot of other things next. He was going to suffer from being grounded all day, and the cause of his suffering was the ants. So they were going to pay. He tried salt, rubbing alcohol and water, none of which did anything.

Then he did something he knew was wrong. His parents would ground him for a year if they caught him, but he boiled some water and poured that on the ants. They died instantly. Then he grabbed some hydrogen peroxide from the bathroom.

Although the boiling water was the most effective, the hydrogen peroxide was the most impressive. Jason poured about a tablespoon of it onto one corner of the farm. Within seconds of the liquid splashing onto them, the ants began to shake and dance as if they were being electrocuted. They lost all sense of direction and ran around in crazy patterns. Their legs seemed to be going in different directions at the same time. Then they kind of wound themselves into a circle, twitched a little while longer and died. Jason thought it was great.

He spent a couple of hours torturing the ants before he got bored. Then he went and found his dad in the garage.

"Dad?" he asked quietly.

His father looked over at him from the workbench.

Jason tried to look as humble as he could. "I know it was mean of me to say that Brian's gift was dumb. I guess I was hoping for something else."

Jason's father put one elbow on the workbench and studied Jason. "Why the change of heart? Getting bored?"

Jason abandoned the humble approach. "Can't I please go over to Eddie's house?" he begged. "I won't complain about anybody's gift from now on."

His father looked at his watch. Then he turned back to his project. "All right," he said. Then he turned his head quickly and looked seriously at Jason. "Don't do it again," he warned in a tone of voice that Jason knew from past experience to be an Ultimate Order.

"Okay." He tore out of the garage and ran down the street to the fort. He spent the rest of the afternoon playing with his friends and forgot all about his ants.

Late in the day, he came back just in time to wash up and have dinner. After that he took his shower. He didn't even look at the ant farm until that evening.

The ants had been busy while he was out. They had re-dug their tunnels. Jason looked at the tunnels, but there was something strange about the way they were laid out, even something familiar.

Suddenly, he realized what was so familiar. An icy chill swept through his body, taking his breath with it. He took a step closer, unable to believe what he was seeing.

The dead-end tunnels and oddly shaped burrows formed letters! They spelled out a simple word: H–A–T–E.

Jason's jaw began to ache, and he realized his teeth were clamped tightly shut. He stared at the ants a moment longer, then ran to the bathroom. He grabbed the bottle of hydrogen peroxide from the shelf, but his hands were shaking so badly he dropped it.

"Jason?" he heard his mother call from the kitchen. "What are you doing?"

"Nothing, Mom," he managed to yell back. He snatched up the bottle and ran back to his room, biting his lip to keep from screaming.

Breathing heavily, he stalked toward the ant farm. When he reached the front of his dresser, he unscrewed the cap off the bottle. Then, with great determination, he slowly poured the hydrogen peroxide over the whole farm.

As the deathly liquid washed over the ants, they burst into convulsive frenzy. Their bodies jittered and danced across the soil as the peroxide burned its way into their systems. Jason watched without pity as the liquid seeped down into the tunnels.

Then he shuddered, and looked around the room as if he didn't recognize it. The ant farm was half filled with liquid, and hundreds of ants were thrashing out their deaths. With a sob, he set the bottle down. Then, as cautiously as he would touch a snarling dog, he picked up the farm. He held it at arm's length as he snuck through the house and out to the trash cans in the backyard. Into the trash it went. Then he ran back inside.

As soon as he had calmed down and caught his breath, he went to the living room. "'Night, Mom," he said, kissing her on the cheek. "'Night, Dad."

His parents wished him good night, and he returned to his room. Climbing into bed, lying back on his pillow, he tried to think about anything but the ant farm.

But he couldn't. "That wasn't real," he whispered to himself. He kept thinking that over and over, until finally he fell into a troubled sleep.

Late that night, he woke up suddenly. His skin felt funny. He reached over and turned on the small reading lamp on his nightstand.

In the sudden light, he was puzzled to see that his arm was black from some kind of stain. And it felt as if it were on fire. Then, with a mental click that made him dizzy, he realized that his arm was covered with ants! His breath came in short gasps as his head creaked around to look at his chest. A grotesque nightshirt of black ants covered his chest, each angry creature chewing at his flesh with its tiny jaws.

Jason's thoughts spun out of control. He tried to scream. But a wave of ants swarmed into his mouth, blocking his voice forever.

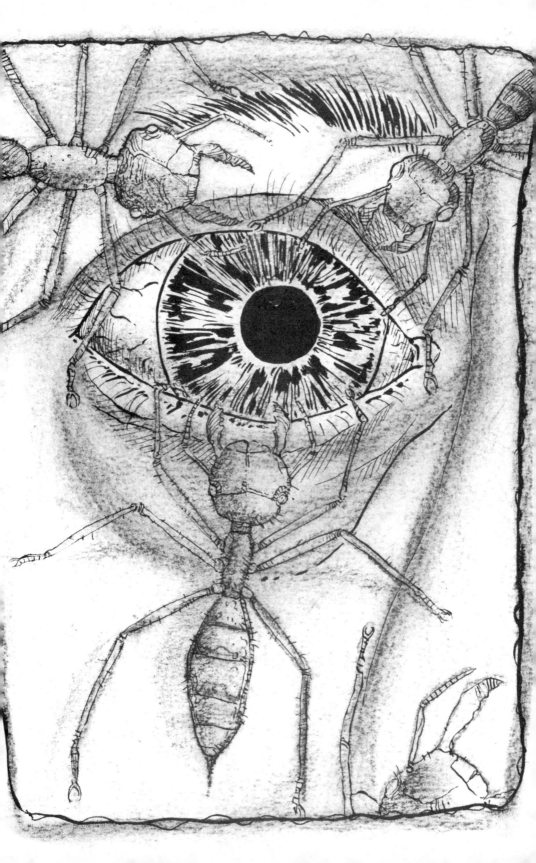

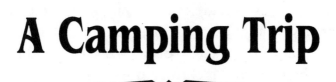

A Camping Trip

The bus pulled away with fourteen yelling boys inside. Alex waved to his mom and dad from the rear window, then squeezed in between his two friends, Darrel and Kent.

"Can you believe it?" asked Darrel. "Mr. Kane is actually taking us hiking." Alex and Kent shook their heads in agreement as the three boys looked toward the front of the bus at their science teacher.

Mr. Kane had only just begun teaching at their school, and he was not very popular. He was going bald, and a fringe of reddish hair circled the base of his skull from ear to ear. His huge stomach always seemed to peek out between the buttons of his shirt. He wore thick black plastic glasses, and one of the boys had seen him smoking a pipe once. In class, he never laughed or made jokes. In fact, he never said anything that didn't have to do with science, and he kept to himself when he had lunchroom duty.

The drive took the entire morning. Just after noon, they pulled into a small parking area deep in the forest. Mr. Kane led the boys off the bus.

"From here, we will follow the trail in for approximately one mile," he told them while they ate their lunches. "Then it branches, and we will follow the upper trail until we hit camp." When everybody was ready, the group set off.

Late in the day they came to a small lake. To one side was a grassy meadow filled with little white flowers. The rest of the lake was ringed by pine trees.

Mr. Kane led the class to the meadow, where they gratefully shrugged off their packs. "Now," he announced, "before any of you go off exploring, I want your tents set up. Then we will gather firewood, and I will prepare the meal." Alex groaned along with the rest of the boys. But Mr. Kane insisted.

As they unrolled tents and sorted through the poles and ropes, they heard the soft clip-clop, clip-clop of hoofbeats. After a moment, a man rode out of the trees on horseback. He saw the class and headed over to them.

He was younger than Mr. Kane, and was tall and thin, with a friendly smile. He wore jeans and a green flannel shirt with a Forestry Service patch on the sleeve. A cowboy hat was pushed back on his head.

"Hi, guys," he waved.

"Who are you?" asked Mr. Kane, stepping forward.

"Park Ranger. You in charge here?"

Mr. Kane nodded. By this time, most of the boys were crowded around the visitor, petting his horse.

"Well, if you need anything, my station is up that trail over there." He pointed to the far side of the lake, where a trail followed an inlet up the mountain. "I've got a fire lookout up there."

"Hey, mister?" said Billy. "Is that some kind of a gun?" He was pointing to a black, futuristic-looking device that was sticking out of the horse's saddlebag.

"Well, sort of," the ranger laughed. He reached into the bag and pulled out the strange object.

"This is a crossbow. It's a bit different from a normal bow, as you can see. Crossbows came along about 400 years after the bow and arrow. Basically, you just put a bow on a stock, like a rifle." He reached into the saddlebag and drew out something that looked like an arrow, but was shorter and had a pointed tip instead of an arrowhead. "Then you use a special kind of arrow called a bolt. It fits into this groove here on the top of the stock." He placed the bolt on top of the crossbow. "Then you aim it like a gun and pull the trigger."

"How far can you shoot it?" asked Darrel.

"Oh, couple hundred yards, I suppose."

"Show us!" the boys yelled.

"Can't do it," the ranger said, laughing. "I don't like to waste my bolts on trees and rocks. You never know when you'll run into a dangerous animal." He put the crossbow away and grabbed the reins. "Take care, guys. Have a good time."

The boys waved good-bye, disappointed, but they had plenty to talk about after the ranger's visit.

After a dinner of hot dogs and beans, Mr. Kane made them wash their dishes. It was getting dark fast—too late to do any exploring—but Mr. Kane was building a fire, and roasting marshmallows and telling spooky stories sounded just as fun. They sat around the fire, still talking excitedly about the ranger and his crossbow. Then, to everyone's surprise, Mr. Kane spoke up.

"Are any of you familiar with the story of the Lothan boys?"

They all shook their heads.

"Jeremy, Donald and James were three brothers," he began. "One day Jeremy was hiking around and saw something sticking up out of the ground. It looked like it might be the shriveled side of a dead tree trunk. Jeremy dug around it to see for sure. He kept digging and digging—but suddenly he shrunk back in horror. It was a head! An old mummified Indian head! It was then that he realized he was on ancient Indian burial ground. . . .You know, the Indians used to roam these very mountains, long before the white man came."

Alex had a brief moment of surprise as he realized that Mr. Kane was a really good storyteller. All of the boys were quiet, listening intently as first the mummy was dug up and brought to the brothers' secret fort, then as it came to life and killed Jeremy.

"The younger brothers, James and Donald, tried to escape," Mr. Kane continued, "but the mummy grabbed

Donald and lifted him off the floor. Donald kicked and squirmed, but he couldn't break loose. As James watched in horror, the mummy plunged its hand into Donald's chest and tore his heart out. James dove through the doorway and ran down that mountain like he had never run before. And he made it. But he never found out what happened to the monster. And he never, ever came back into these mountains again."

At the end of the story, Alex shivered. Mr. Kane told an excellent story! All of the other boys seemed equally surprised.

Mr. Kane looked around and smiled. "All right, men," he said, standing. "Time for bed." He watched while everyone got ready. "And don't wander off in the middle of the night," he warned as they crawled into their tents.

The next morning was sunny and warm. By the time Alex got dressed, some of the other boys were up. Mr. Kane had already started a fire and was serving breakfast.

"Martin," he said, "could you please wake up Bret? Tell him he is going to miss breakfast if he doesn't hurry up."

Martin walked over and pulled back the tent flap. "Mr. Kane! He's not here!" he cried, turning to the others.

Mr. Kane stood up and walked over, surrounded by the rest of the boys. Bret's sleeping bag was open, but there was no sign of the boy. Mr. Kane looked around the clearing, then he called out, "Bret! Bret!"

Within moments, all the other boys were shouting Bret's name too. But there was no answer.

Mr. Kane turned to face the boys. "All right. Clean up your dishes. Then form into pairs."

With excited speed they did as he said. One boy, Kent, was left alone.

"Kent," said Mr. Kane calmly, "you stay with me. The rest of you split up and search around the lake for Bret. If you find him and he is hurt, one of you stay with him and the other come back here to get me. Understand?"

The boys nodded.

"Please do not go too far," he cautioned. "And pay attention to the direction you are going so you can find your way back to camp."

Alex and Darrel decided to go search the far side of the lake. They searched for over an hour, with no luck. When it was nearly ten o'clock, they thought it was best to get back to the campsite. Mr. Kane was there, with the rest of the other boys. None of them had found any trace of Bret either.

"Hey, Mr. Kane?" asked Darrel. "Where's Kent?"

Mr. Kane looked at him strangely. "He went to find you and Alex. Isn't he with you?"

Darrel and Alex shook their heads. Alex felt very cold all of a sudden. The rest of the boys were quiet. Then John slowly raised his hand.

"Mr. Kane," he asked quietly, "you don't suppose something's happened to them, do you?"

That was exactly what Alex was thinking, but he joined the other boys in teasing John. "What do you think? A monster ate them?" He laughed nervously.

Mr. Kane held up his hand. "Quiet down, boys." He turned to John. "That is a very good question. But I'm not sure, so I want all of you to stay here while I hike to the ranger station and radio for help." He looked around at each of the boys. "Stay together, you understand? I should be back within two hours."

They all nodded quietly. Mr. Kane picked up a small pack and started walking. As soon as he was out of sight, the class exploded into excited questions.

"I don't care what you guys think," John said loudly. "This is weird."

"Oh, come on," said Doug. "Bret probably fell down the mountain!"

"Well, what about Kent?" asked Darrel.

"Who knows?" answered Billy. "Maybe he went to see the ranger. Maybe he got lost."

"Lost?" Alex yelled. "How do you get lost walking around a lake?"

"What happened then?" Billy yelled back.

At that, all of the boys started yelling back and forth. Then Martin's voice cut through them all.

"What about Mr. Kane?" he asked.

Alex felt a small shiver twitch through his body. He wished Martin hadn't said that. The rest of the boys stared at Martin.

"Why not?" he continued. "Did you see the way he looked when I told him Bret's tent was empty? He wasn't even surprised!" He looked around him. "Maybe he's not even going to the ranger station. Maybe he's out there right now—watching us."

"No way!" Alex shouted. "That's crazy. Mr. Kane is a *teacher!*"

"Yeah?" asked Doug. "For how long? He's only been at Golden Oak for one semester. He could be anyone!"

"Yeah," agreed Darrel, turning to Alex. "Remember? Kent didn't think he was the kind of person who'd want to go camping. Unless," he said slowly, looking at all of them, "unless he's not really here to camp."

Alex shook his head violently. His friends were building a strong case. But he still couldn't believe it.

"Then why would he wait until now to kill one of us?" Doug asked.

Alex was relieved someone was coming to Mr. Kane's defense.

"And why do it this way?" Doug continued. "What are people going to do when we get back and two kids are missing? There'll be cops all over the place!"

"Who says any of us will get back?" asked John, quietly. "Maybe none of us will; and Mr. Kane will just drive on to the next school."

Alex didn't know whether to laugh, scream or cry. He was breathing heavily, and cold sweat was running down his sides. He looked around. "Then what do we do?" he asked.

Nobody answered, and he continued. "Do we hike out? What if it's not Mr. Kane? Then what happens? What if Mr. Kane gets back here with the ranger and we're all gone? What if Kent shows up and finds everybody gone? What then?"

"But what if it is Mr. Kane?" added Alan. "Then what? Do we just sit here and wait for him to pick us off?"

Once again, the air was split by twelve shouting voices. Darrel pulled Alex aside.

"Alex. What do you really think is going on?"

"I—I don't know. Mr. Kane did bring us here." Alex looked at their friends. Everyone looked scared. Martin looked like he was ready to cry, and Alex felt like he wanted to also. He turned back to Darrel. In a very low voice he said, "Do you think we should go to the ranger station ourselves?"

Darrel stared at him. "Are you crazy?" he finally asked.

"I don't know what else to do! I think if the two of us go it'll be okay."

Darrel thought about it, then took a deep breath. "All right," he decided. "Let's do it."

They told the others that they planned to hike to the ranger station for help. There was a shocked silence, but nobody else offered to come.

"Do either of you guys know how to get there?" asked Doug, finally.

"Well, the ranger said it was just up the trail at the end of the lake," answered Alex. "I guess we'll just follow it until we get to the station."

Alex and Darrel set off. They made their way around the lake, then, with Darrel in the lead, they started climbing.

The trees grew thick and tall along the trail, and the afternoon sun barely filtered its way through the needles of the pines. They walked in silence. Alex barely watched the trail. He spent most of the time turning his head this way and that, trying to look in a hundred directions at one time.

"How much farther could it be?" he asked after a while.

"I don't know," panted Darrel. "Maybe he meant it wasn't far on horseback."

Alex looked at the sky. "I just hope we find it before it

gets dark."

"What if we don't?" Darrel asked. "What if we're nowhere near it, and Mr. Kane has been following us all along?"

"Shut up!" hissed Alex. "I think—"

Alex never told Darrel what he thought because just then they heard a noise. They froze and listened as hard as they could.

It came again. Someone, or something, was walking down the trail! The two boys stood still for a moment, paralyzed with fear. Then, at almost the same time, they dove off to the side of the trail and hid among the trees.

The footsteps grew louder. Alex looked from his hiding place over at Darrel, whose eyes bulged with terror. Tears were running down his face.

Then a shape appeared out of the gloom. It took a moment for Alex to realize it, but then he felt a relief so intense he thought he would fall down. It was the ranger!

The boys burst back onto the trail from their hiding places. The ranger stopped, surprise on his face. He held the crossbow in one hand, and wore a pack on his back.

"Mr. Ranger!" Alex practically screamed. "Boy, am I glad to see . . . ," his voice trailed off as his throat tightened in fear. The ranger started to smile.

"Hey," said Darrel from behind him. "That looks like Mr. Kane's pack!"

The entire forest seemed to hold its breath as Alex watched a small drop of blood fall silently from the loaded crossbow to the ground.

Mummy's Little Helper

Anne lay in bed with the sheets pulled up under her chin. Her ears felt like they were sticking straight out from her head, she was listening so hard. Her eyes stared into the darkness of her bedroom.

Then she heard it again. A high, whispery voice that seemed to come from the walls around her.

"Anne," the voice breathed. "Help me."

Anne whimpered and pulled the cover over her head. After a moment's thought, she stuck her head back out again to watch the room. Then, just like the night before, she heard soft sobbing flow around her like air. Except last night she had run into her parents' room and spent the night huddled between the two of them in their bed. That was when she found out that, for some reason, they were unable to hear The Voice.

Tonight she asked quietly, "Who are you?"

The sobbing stopped. Anne's breathing stopped too. She waited for an answer.

"Help me," the voice begged again.

"*Where* are you?" Anne asked, slightly louder. There was no reply. She waited for an answer, but none came. Still scared, but also a little disappointed, she soon fell asleep.

The next day at school, she pulled her friend Robin aside on the playground.

"My bedroom is haunted," she announced abruptly.

Robin stared at her. "What do you mean?"

Anne looked over her shoulder to make sure there was no one around. "The last two nights," she whispered, "I've heard a voice coming from my walls."

Robin's mouth dropped open. "What?" She looked at Anne as if she were speaking a different language.

"I know it sounds really weird. But I swear! The voice is really soft, but kind of whiny. Like a little kid's."

"What does it say?"

"It just keeps asking me to help it."

"What?"

Anne threw her hands up. "I know! It keeps saying, 'Help me,'" she mimicked in a whispering voice. "And it knows my name. I'm really starting to get scared."

"Have you told your parents?"

Anne shook her head. "No. I mean, I tried, but they can't hear it. Maybe only kids can hear it. Besides, I'm not even sure it's real." She looked at her friend in desperation, hoping Robin would tell her she wasn't going crazy.

Robin just shook her head and looked puzzled.

Anne continued. "I want you to help me figure out what's going on."

"Me?" Robin took a step back. "How?"

"I already asked my mom if you could spend the night tonight. If you stay, then we'll see if you can hear it too."

Robin looked around her as if she were trying to get away. "I don't know, Anne."

"Please! You're my best friend!"

Robin thought about it for a moment. "All right," she agreed uneasily. "But I hope we don't hear anything!"

That night the two girls huddled under the covers of Anne's bed together.

"What do you think it is?" Robin asked.

Anne thought a moment. "I think it's the ghost of some poor kid who died here."

"Maybe the house was built over some old Indian graveyard, like in *Poltergeist*," Robin suggested.

"Do you think it could be the house itself talking?" Anne wondered.

Their excited whispers soon became yawns as the night wore on. Anne had tried to keep Robin from falling asleep, but with no luck.

She stared sleepily at the ceiling. *I don't know if I want to hear The Voice again or not,* she thought. *But what if it's the ghost of some poor little girl, just like me. Maybe—*

"Anne," the voice called. "Help me."

Anne's eyes snapped open, and she pushed at Robin's

shoulder. Her friend turned over and started to speak. Anne quickly put one hand over Robin's mouth, and with the other held a finger to her lips.

"Help me!" the voice pleaded.

Robin's eyes grew so wide Anne thought they'd pop out of her head. She sat up and pulled Anne's hand away. "Where is it coming from?" she whispered. She was so scared her voice was almost as high as the ghostly one.

Anne shook her head violently. She put her mouth next to Robin's ear. "I don't know."

They both strained their ears.

"Help me," the voice cried, beginning to sob.

"Come on," whispered Anne. "Let's see if we can hear it anywhere else in the house."

"Are you crazy!" Robin hissed.

"Come on!" Anne urged. She slipped out of bed and practically pulled Robin out too.

"Anne, I don't think this is a good idea."

Anne waved her to be silent. This was beginning to be more interesting than scary. Maybe they would solve some ancient mystery! They crept into the hallway. The sobbing seemed louder there.

"Can't your parents hear this?" asked Robin.

"Uh-uh," said Anne, pulling her friend down the hall after her. As they approached the kitchen, the sobbing seemed to grow louder. It no longer seemed to come from the walls but now carried up from the floor beneath them. Suddenly Anne whirled and faced Robin.

"I know where it's coming from!"

"Where?"

"The basement!"

Robin stared at the floor. "Should we tell your mom and dad?"

Anne thought about that. It was one thing to have an adventure. But it was another to get in trouble for doing it—and they would if they woke her parents up. It would be more exciting to solve the mystery all on their own.

"Let's just go take a look," she finally decided. "If it's something bad, we'll go get my mom and dad."

Robin studied her friend. "All right," she agreed after a moment. Then she shook her head. "I can't believe we're doing this!"

They crept through the kitchen to the utility room. Anne grabbed a flashlight from one of the drawers and led Robin over to the basement door. With a deep breath, she pulled the door open and shone the light in.

The sobs seemed to fill the room. They were definitely louder here than anywhere else in the house.

Anne turned on the basement light. With the glare of the bare light bulb, the sobbing stopped. Anne and Robin stood on the top steps and examined the room. There was nothing there that was out of the ordinary. A long table stood against one wall, where Anne's father kept all his tools. Off in one corner was the water heater, and next to that was a cedar closet where her mom kept some old clothes. The furnace took up the other corner.

Anne descended a few more steps and looked around. She glanced up at Robin. Then she walked all the way down into the basement. The floor was made of long wooden planks laid over the bare earth.

"There's nothing here," she announced, somewhat surprised.

"Are you sure?" asked Robin from the stairs.

Anne nodded. "Yeah. Come on down."

Robin stepped cautiously down to the basement floor. "It sure sounded like it was coming from down here."

Anne turned to answer. "Yeah, it really—"

"Help me," the voice broke in.

She had been right! There was someone down here! Anne's blood was racing. She barely noticed that Robin was about to scream.

"Help me, Anne," the child's voice begged. The voice

had come from under the floorboards! But how could something live under there? Was there a cave or something?

"Anne," warned Robin in a cracking voice. "Don't!"

Anne frowned at her friend. "Look," she said, pointing to the wooden planks. "I'll bet you someone's buried under there. And now they need help. They need to have a decent burial."

Robin felt like she was going to throw up. "Anne," she pleaded with her friend. "Let's get your parents. Or the police. Or someone!" She started to back away toward the stairs.

Anne was too excited to stop. She felt like a detective

solving an important case. She strode over to her father's tools and grabbed a chisel and hammer. She looked up at Robin.

"You don't have to stay if you're afraid. But close the door behind you so I don't wake up my parents."

Robin climbed the stairs and closed the door. She sat down on the steps, too worried to leave her friend alone.

Anne attacked the boards in front of the stairway. She managed to get the chisel under the edge of one of the planks and, using the hammer, was able to pry it up. A dark space was revealed.

She sat back and studied the hole. Did she really want to do this? Then she grabbed the flashlight and beamed it into the opening.

Under the floorboards was a small, shallow grave scooped out of the dirt. And huddled in the bottom was the mummified body of a small child.

"I was right!" Anne said triumphantly, looking up at Robin.

Robin peered down at Anne. She heard a dry sound, like two pieces of paper being rubbed together. Then she gasped—a brown, flaking arm had shot out of the hole! Robin's stomach seemed to jump to the back of her mouth as she watched the thing drag her kicking friend into the hole with incredible strength.

A horrible thought thrust into her mind like an icicle—that when something calls for help, it might be because it's hungry. Then her mind stopped working and she sat on the steps and screamed.

Shadow Play

David stood in the middle of his new room, looking at all the cardboard boxes. He kicked at one. He still hadn't gotten used to the move. In fact, he wished his dad had never gotten the new job.

"Don't just stand there, David," said his mother from the doorway. "Start putting your stuff away."

David opened the nearest box and pulled out some clothes. He knew his parents were excited about the new house, so he tried not to be too mad. But it just wasn't fair. He would never see any of his friends again, and who knew what the kids in the new school would be like?

He finished unpacking and decided to go out front. That

was one nice thing about the new house—it had a front yard to play in. It was a pretty good-sized lawn, with a hedge along the sides. And some bushes and ivy grew along the front of the house. There were probably some good spiders to be found in this yard, he thought as he poked through the ivy.

"What'cha doing?" came a voice from behind him. David sat up and turned to see another boy on the sidewalk. He had stopped his bicycle and was watching David.

"Just goofing around," David answered.

"My name's Greg. I live over there." He pointed down the street. "What's your name?"

"David."

"This your house?"

"Uh-huh. We just moved in."

"Too bad," pronounced Greg, shaking his head.

David looked at him in shock. "What do you mean?"

Now it was Greg who looked shocked. "Didn't your parents tell you?"

David shook his head.

Greg laid his bike down and came over to crouch by David.

"The family who lived here before yours," he whispered, "disappeared without a trace!"

"What?" David said with disbelief. He watched Greg closely, certain he'd start laughing any second.

But Greg just shrugged. "Nobody knows. It was a mom, a dad and their son. They lived here about ten years. Weird family. Really mean."

"But where did they go?"

Greg shrugged again. "You see, one night there was a really big storm. I remember 'cause I thought our roof was going to blow off. There was lightning and thunder, and it was raining buckets. All the lights went out too."

"Yeah," said David. "So?" He was getting impatient.

"So the next morning the storm was gone. But the front door of this house was wide open. My dad and some other grown-ups checked it out, and there was nobody home!"

David sat back, relieved. "Big deal. They probably left on vacation and forgot to close the door."

Greg stood up angrily. "Yeah? Well, they never came back, and their car was still here!"

Just then they both heard Greg's mother calling to him.

"I gotta go." He stood up and mounted his bike. "Good luck," he wished David before pedaling away.

That night at dinner David asked his parents if they knew what had happened to the people who had lived there before them.

"No," said his father. "What have you heard?"

"Some kid from down the street told me the family left one night and never came back."

David saw his dad and mom look at each other and quickly look away.

"Well, David," his father said, "the lady who sold us the house said they moved away."

"What if they come back and want their house?"

"They won't." His father smiled. "The house is ours now."

Later that night, after going to bed, David heard his mom and dad arguing in the living room. He slipped quietly out of bed and crept into the hallway.

" . . . you're not worried?" he heard his mother say.

"I'm sure it will never go any further," his dad answered.

"But who knows *what* those kids will be telling David."

"Honey," his father answered, "I sincerely doubt that those kids' fathers went home and told them there was blood sprayed all over the place."

"Shhh! David might hear!"

"All right," his father said in a lower voice. "Look, I really don't think there's anything to worry about, okay? I'm sure David has heard all he ever will about the house."

"I hope you're right."

They fell silent, and after a moment the television came on. David snuck back to his room and lay in bed. His mind was racing. Blood? Wow! A mystery! This house might turn out to be pretty cool, after all. What had happened here? He stared at the dark corner of his room and thought of old horror movies he had watched.

But what was that?

David thought he saw something move in the darkness. His breathing stopped as he tried to convince himself that he hadn't seen anything. He had thought that corner was empty; hadn't it been when he climbed into bed? He sat up slowly, staring at the corner. He could hear the television in the other room.

Then he saw it again. In the darkest corner of his room, something moved. But there wasn't anything there—was there? No, it was more like the *darkness itself* had moved! He sucked in his breath and glanced at his nightstand. A small bedside lamp stood there, next to the clock.

With a moan, David shot his hand out and switched on the small lamp. The yellow light filled the room, and in the corner was . . . nothing. His heart pounding, David looked around. There was nothing out of place, nothing that shouldn't have been there.

Had he really seen something? He studied every inch of his room to make sure there was nothing there. Then he slowly settled back down into bed and stared at the corner until his eyelids grew heavy and fell over his eyes.

The next morning, his father came in to wake him. As David rubbed the sleep out of his eyes, his father switched off the bedside lamp.

"Did you forget to turn the light off?" he asked David.

"Uh, yeah," David answered. "Sorry, Dad."

All that day, he tried to forget what had happened the night before. It was ridiculous, he told himself. He was really being a baby; he hadn't been afraid of the dark since he was a little kid! No, he must have been half asleep and imagining things.

That night, however, after his parents tucked him in, he wasn't so sure anymore. Gathering his courage, he turned off his bedside lamp and sat back on his pillow. There was enough light coming from the living room to fill his room with pale shadows. His eyes darted from side to side, watching.

Then his room seemed to grow suddenly colder. In the inky blackness under his desk, there was movement. David's eyes locked onto the spot. His breath came faster. There was nothing there! There couldn't be!

Then it moved again. It was shapeless, like a blob. And

it didn't move like an animal. It flowed like water. Out from under the desk and straight for the foot of his bed!

David screamed and shot his hand out to switch on the light.

The electric glare drove the shadow back, where it pooled on the floor under his desk.

"What's the matter, honey?" asked his mother as she ran into the room. His father was right beside her.

"I . . . I thought I saw something move over there," David's voice broke. "Under the desk."

David's father flipped on the room light, banishing the shadows. He knelt down and looked under the desk. "There's nothing here," he announced.

"The shadow," David insisted. "The shadow was moving."

His mother sat on the edge of the bed and smoothed his hair. "You were having a bad dream, dear."

David opened his mouth to argue, then realized it was useless. His parents would never believe him. And in the bright light of the ceiling lamp, he wasn't sure he believed it either. It sure had seemed real, though.

"Yeah," he said. "I guess so. Sorry."

His mother smiled and got up. "That's okay." His father stood up too.

"Night, kiddo," he said, turning to leave. As he walked out, he flipped off the room light.

David watched the shadows reappear. "Dad! Can I leave the room light on? Please?"

His father looked annoyed but turned the light back on. The shadows fled.

"Sweet dreams, honey," his mother wished him. Then his parents left the room.

For the next few nights, he slept with his room light on. He knew his father was less than pleased about it. One day he heard them in the kitchen, talking about his "fear of the dark." They were both worried about him, and his father thought it was "nonsense."

David walked slowly back to his room and sat on the bed. Maybe his dad was right. He was too old to be afraid of the dark. But it seemed too real to be a nightmare.

That night he resolved to do something about it. When his parents came to tuck him in, he said, "I'd like to try sleeping with the lights off."

"Are you sure?" his mother asked. He nodded.

"All right," she said. His father stood over him and ruffled his hair.

"Good night," he said. "It'll be okay." They left the room, and David closed his eyes.

David woke suddenly from a deep sleep. He didn't know what had woken him. Then he remembered: his light was off! A shiver danced over his skin like cold water being poured on him. He slowly sat up in bed. He looked toward the corner of his room. In the faint light cast by the street lamp outside, he could see an enormous shadow stretched halfway up the wall.

It had no definite shape, but flickered and shifted like black fire. A small voice in the back of David's mind tried to tell him it was just the shadow of . . . of a tree or something. But then, as if the shadow knew he had seen it, it rushed toward him. He screamed and threw himself toward his

bedside lamp. His numb fingers fumbled with the switch as he kicked himself out of his bed sheets. Just as the shadow was reaching his bed, the light flared on.

His parents came running into the room.

"What is it?" his mother asked. His father stood in the doorway, with a strange expression on his face.

David babbled out the story through his tears. "The shadow. It almost got me!"

His mother held him and tried to calm him down. "It's all right, now. We're here. Don't worry."

David wondered if he was going crazy. He knew his parents probably thought so, which made him feel worse. He finally calmed down, but only after talking his parents into leaving the light on before they went back to bed.

The next day dawned gray and drizzly and grew quickly worse. Thick, black clouds rolled in to cover the sun. The wind began to blow hard, and David watched his father lock all the patio furniture in the garage.

Then, with a flash of lightning and crash of thunder, the rain began. Huge drops shot down from the sky and shattered against the ground. The windows rattled with every gust of wind, and it looked as if somebody were washing them down with a hose. The sound of the rain pelting against the pavement outside was loud enough to be heard inside the house.

Since four o'clock, the sky had been pitch-black. David was huddled on the couch with his mom, watching television. His dad sat in his chair, reading. David was glad to be inside on a night like this. A blast of lightning lit the sky, and the thunder that followed seemed to shake the house. David crawled further under the blanket with his mom. Gusts of wind pushed at the house.

Suddenly, the room went dark. David heard his father mutter something. Then he said louder, "Electricity's out."

To David, those two words seemed to stop his heart. No electricity! That meant no lights! He hugged his mother tightly and whispered, "What are we gonna do?"

"It's all right, David," she said. "We've got candles and a flashlight."

David heard his father get up. "Where are the candles?" he asked.

"In the third drawer in the kitchen," his mother answered. His dad went to find them while his mother held David.

"It's all right, David," she said again.

"But the shadows—"

His mother sighed softly. "Tell you what. Why don't you sleep with me and your dad tonight, okay?"

David felt weak with relief. "Okay, Mom."

David's father came back with a lit candle stuck to a plate. "Flashlight's dead," he announced. "I can't even remember the last time we used it."

"Well," said his mom, "shall we go to bed, then? I told David he could sleep with us tonight."

David's father didn't say anything right away. "Yeah, okay," he finally answered. "Let's hit the sack."

As the three of them walked past David's bedroom, he glanced in. It was there! "Mom," he whispered. "Look! See the shadow moving?"

"Honey, it's the candlelight that does that."

David bit his lip. Then he nodded. Yeah, he told himself, it could be the candles. Still, he hurried into his mom and dad's room.

His dad set the candle on his bedside table. His mom lit another one and set it on the dresser.

"Mom?" David asked. "Can we leave a candle lit?"

He saw his mother look at his dad.

"Don't you feel safe with us?" she asked.

David squirmed. "Yes, but—" Greg's story flashed through his mind. "Just can we?" He begged her with his eyes.

"Okay, honey. We'll leave one on the dresser, okay?"

"Thanks, Mom." David hugged her. Then he hugged his father, too. After a second, his dad hugged him back.

His parents fell asleep quickly. But David was too frightened to sleep. He lay there watching the shadows. Did they move because of the unsteady candlelight? The occasional flash of lightning that lit the room drove them away. But only for a moment. They quickly came back, bobbing and weaving around the walls and ceiling. David watched as long as he could, but his eyelids grew heavy and he fell asleep.

There was a noise.

"What was that?" his mother asked, startled.

"I don't know," said his father as he threw the covers back. David had also woken up at the sound. But his eyes were riveted to the candle.

It had burned very low, almost to the base. Even as he watched, it began to sputter. His dad was out of bed and was tying a robe around his waist. His mother was watching anxiously. The shadows loomed over the bed.

Then the candle went out. David heard his father cursing as he looked for the matches. "Hurry, Dad," David tried to shout. But it came out as a whisper. "Hurry!" he sobbed.

Suddenly, a match flared. David saw his father standing by the bed. His father smiled at him. David's smile turned to wide-eyed horror as the hands of his father's shadow wrapped around his dad's neck. His father dropped the lit match and grabbed at the dark claws.

David turned to his mother as a scream worked its way up his throat. His mother lay very still, a dark shadow where her face should have been. He whipped his gaze back to his father, who now hung from his shadow's grasp.

David's mind seemed to explode in fear, and he looked up and screamed. In the last light of the dying match, he saw a child-sized shadow drop toward him from the ceiling.

The Dollhouse

obody really liked Jenny very much. On the other hand, that was probably because nobody knew anything about her, Karen thought as they walked to Jenny's house.

Karen still remembered when Jenny walked into the classroom on the first day of school. She seemed to creep in, as if she were afraid somebody would notice her. She came in and sat in the back of the room and didn't talk to anyone the whole day. In fact, if Ms. Henry, the teacher, hadn't made the whole class sit in alphabetical order, Karen probably never would have actually talked to her. But because Jenny's last name was Victor and Karen's was Wells, they sat next to each other in the rear of the room.

The first time Karen had tried to talk to her neighbor she had little success. "Hi," she had introduced herself that first day. "I'm Karen."

Jenny just nodded. "Hello," she said quietly. That was all she said.

Looking back on that as they walked to Jenny's, Karen smiled. That was probably as far as things would have gone if it hadn't been for the elephant.

Karen loved to collect miniatures. She was always getting her parents to buy her tiny tea sets and tiny chairs and things. One day, she brought a little carved elephant to show Kelly, her best friend, at recess. It was made of wood and was perfectly detailed, down to the two little nose holes at the end of the trunk.

After recess, Karen put the little carving on her desk. It wasn't until halfway through class that she noticed that Jenny kept sneaking glances at the elephant.

When the bell rang for lunch, Jenny turned toward her shyly. "May I see your elephant?" she asked quietly.

Karen felt thrilled that Jenny was finally opening up. "Sure. But be careful. I just got it, and my parents would kill me if something happened to it."

Jenny held the delicate carving in the palm of her hand and stared at it. "It's beautiful," she said.

"Do you like things like this?" Karen asked her.

Jenny nodded, still staring at the tiny pachyderm.

"I've got a whole collection of stuff like this," Karen continued. "And my step-dad gave me these really neat miniatures from Asia. Villages carved inside eggshells and things like that. If you want, you can come over and see them."

Jenny slowly put the elephant back on Karen's desk. She seemed to be thinking about it. Then she looked up at Karen and smiled. "Thank you. I'd like that."

Karen shrugged. "Sure. No problem. How 'bout tomorrow after school?"

Jenny smiled again as she got up. "Okay," she said, and left the room. Karen carefully rewrapped the elephant in tissue paper, and put it in a matchbox. Then she went to lunch also.

Her friend Kelly was waiting for her, anxious to talk. "I don't believe it," she said, nodding toward where Jenny sat, alone. "You actually got her to talk. What did she say?"

"She really liked my elephant," Karen answered, still somewhat surprised at Jenny's reaction. "So I told her she could come over to my house tomorrow and see the rest of my collection."

"And? Is she?"

"She said she'd like to. I guess she has to check with her parents, though."

Kelly shook her head. "Why do you try so hard to be everybody's friend?"

"I think she's a nice person. She's just so shy that her own shadow scares her."

The next day, Jenny went to Karen's house after school. Karen's parents weren't home, so the two girls had a snack and Karen showed Jenny her entire collection of miniatures—from elephants and other animals to tiny carriages drawn by prancing horses. The jewel of her collection was the egg. A hole had been cut out of the front of it, and a tiny, delicate village carved out of ivory had been set inside. The inside of the shell had been painted to look like the village was in the mountains, with a powder blue sky above.

"This is beautiful!" Jenny breathed. She stood up and looked shyly at Karen. "I collect miniatures too."

"Oh really? Like what?"

"I brought something with me." She paused. "If you'd like to see it."

Karen smiled. "I'd love to."

Jenny reached into her book bag and pulled out a small wooden box. She placed it on Karen's dresser, making sure to stand it on end. "Open it," she told Karen.

Karen leaned closer and saw that the box was carved to look like a tiny wardrobe. It stood on four little feet, each finely detailed, and it had a wee little knob in the front. Smiling, Karen pinched the doorknob between her thumb and forefinger and opened the closet door.

"Wow!" she gasped. Inside was a whole collection of miniature clothing. There were pants and blouses, simple dresses and elegant gowns. Each one was perfectly made, right down to buttons so small Karen could barely see them. At the bottom of the wardrobe were all different kinds of shoes. Again, each one was perfectly made, as if they were really meant to be worn.

Karen looked at Jenny in amazement. "This is great! Where'd you get this?"

Jenny smiled. "It's from my dollhouse. I thought you might like to see it."

"It's fantastic!" said Karen, turning back to the clothing. Carefully, she plucked out a dress on its hanger and examined it. It was about as long as her finger and looked exactly like a dress of normal size, right down to the zipper up the back. She hung it back in the closet.

"How come you've never brought anything like this to school? You could probably make some friends."

Jenny slowly put the closet away in her bag. "My dolls are my friends," she said quietly.

"That's silly," Karen scoffed. "I'd like to be your friend."

Jenny looked up quickly, and a smile flashed across her face. Then she looked back down at her feet. "I'd like that," she said. "If you'd like, you can come see my dollhouse, too."

Karen didn't take long to decide. Her parents wouldn't be home for another couple of hours. "Is it anything like that closet?"

Jenny smiled. "Oh, yes. It's the best dollhouse in the world!"

Karen laughed. "Then I guess I'll have to!"

And maybe, Karen thought as they walked to Jenny's house, this would help Jenny open up a little more.

Jenny lived in a plain-looking brick house next to a vacant lot. The front lawn was overgrown and brown with a few green patches around the sprinkler heads. There were some ragged bushes along the house, and dried up flowers in pots on the porch. Karen smiled to herself. Her mother, who was a fanatic gardener, would have fainted at the sight of this yard.

Jenny led her up the walk and unlocked the front door.

As she pushed it open, a musty smell floated out.

The inside of the house was filthy. The shades were open, letting the afternoon sun shine through the unwashed windows. There was a layer of dust over everything, and a stack of old TV dinner trays was piled on the coffee table in front of the television. Toys littered the floor.

Karen glanced into the kitchen to her right. It was even worse. Dirty glasses and silverware were everywhere. The wastebasket was crammed to overflowing, and Karen could smell the faint odor of decay.

She wrinkled her nose in disgust. No wonder Jenny was so shy. Her parents must be pigs! She was probably afraid to invite anyone over to her house. She turned to Jenny. "Are your mom and dad at work?"

Jenny shook her head. "No. You'll meet them soon." She looked around the house as if noticing the mess for the first time. Karen could tell Jenny was embarrassed. "Come on," she said quickly, "the dollhouse is back here."

She led Karen into the den. There, in the middle of the room, was the biggest dollhouse Karen had ever seen. It covered almost the entire floor and looked like a small mansion. Karen's mouth dropped open as she moved closer.

A hedge of trees surrounded the huge yard. There was a circular driveway, too, with a gate at either end. Karen knelt down to inspect the house more closely. She vaguely heard Jenny say she would be right back.

Every detail was perfect. Three little brick chimneys poked out of the roof. And someone had even thought to put rain gutters on the roof—with tiny little leaves in them!

Karen moved even closer. The impressive front door had an intricate design of stained glass, with a brass knocker in the middle. Each miniature window had a sill and shutters. The paint was gleaming white with blue trim.

Karen peered in one of the windows. It was a dining room! She gasped in wonder. The room was filled with furniture like the wardrobe Jenny had brought to school. There was a dining table with little plates and napkins set for dinner. A display case like her step-dad's stood to one side, with objects in it that were so small she couldn't even make them out.

She moved on to the next room. It was a living room that was also furnished in exquisite detail. And so were the rest of the rooms on the first floor. There were even tiny little mirrors in the bathrooms!

Karen stood back in amazement. There wasn't a single girl at school who wouldn't die to own this. And here was Jenny, who never even mentioned it!

She leaned forward again and looked into one of the rooms on the second floor. She thought that nothing about this house could further surprise her. But then she saw the people. Seated in an upstairs den were a perfectly carved man and woman. The man was reading a tiny newspaper, and the woman seemed to be knitting. But there was something strange about the woman.

Karen leaned closer. Her heart skipped a beat as she realized what was so strange: the woman's knitting needles were actually moving! She pressed her face against the window—not believing her own eyes—when the woman turned to look at her.

The woman dropped her knitting and stood up. Then the man dropped his paper and ran to the window. Karen threw herself backward. Her head was spinning in confusion, and she seemed to hear a faint, high-pitched whine. This couldn't be real.

"What's the matter?" asked Jenny from behind her.

Karen whirled around to see Jenny standing there with a strange look on her face. "Those people! They moved!"

Jenny cocked her head to one side. "People?" she asked. Then she smiled. "Oh, you must mean my parents! So?"

Karen blinked. She must have heard her incorrectly. But some animal instinct forced her to back slowly away from Jenny. "What do you mean?" she asked in a hoarse voice.

Jenny's smile disappeared. "They wanted to send me away so I shrank them. They're the best part of my collection."

Karen gulped her stomach down. The faint whine seemed to be getting louder. "You're crazy!" she whispered loudly. She felt like she was going to faint. "I'm going home!"

Jenny's eyes narrowed. "I thought you'd like my miniatures," she said accusingly. She took a step forward. "I thought you wanted to be my friend!"

Karen stumbled against the house, caught herself from falling and backed around it. "Get away from me!" she yelled.

She suddenly realized that the noise that had been bothering her was coming from the rear of the dollhouse. Her heart pounding, she glanced down at the backyard of the house.

The little yard was filled with children. They were all looking up at her and screaming in their tiny voices. Her stomach rolled over and her head pounded dully. As her vision turned black, she heard Jenny say, "You're just like all the others. They said they were my friends, too."

Frankenkid

ne night, Jeffrey was watching an old science-fiction movie on television. It was about a man who built a robot to conquer the world. Then, when he died, the robot went crazy and started killing everyone. It was finally turned off by two scientists who found the inventor's notes and deciphered the secret code. As the movie ended, Jeffrey had an idea. He would build a robot! Not to kill people, of course, but to run errands for him and to show off to his friends.

The next morning he began. At first he considered using some plastic blocks he had, but that wouldn't make a strong enough robot. So he pulled his erector set out and began assembling the legs.

Just then, Curtis pushed open the door to Jeffrey's room. "What are you making?" he asked his older brother.

"It's a secret project. I'm not supposed to tell you."

Curtis came closer. "C'mon. What is it?"

Jeffrey laid down the little wrench he was using. "Well, okay. But I'm not sure you're gonna like it."

"What?"

"Mom and Dad asked me to build another son, to replace you."

"Uh-uh!" Curtis yelled, backing up. "You're lying!"

"I told you you wouldn't like it." Jeffrey picked up the wrench and calmly went back to work on his robot's legs. Curtis ran out of the room.

A few minutes later, their mother came in.

"Jeffrey, why did you tell your brother we wanted to replace him?"

"Aw, Mom. I was only joking. How would I know he'd believe a dumb story like that?"

His mother leaned against the doorway, her arms folded. Then she gave him The Look. After a moment, he gave in.

"Okay. I'm sorry. I won't tell him things like that anymore."

"Jeff, I don't know why you say such things in the first place. What *are* you making, anyway?"

"A robot."

"Really? Well, maybe Curtis could help you."

Jeffrey gave his mother his own version of The Look.

"All right," she said, her hand up. "Just stop teasing him all the time."

"Okay, Mom."

Jeffrey closed the door behind her and got back to work. After he finished the two legs, he realized there was a problem: the legs wouldn't bend. How would his robot be able to get around? Then he had an idea. He dove into his closet and pulled out a shoe box full of wheels from old toy cars. He selected eight of them, four for each foot, and began attaching them to the legs.

It took longer than he thought, but he finally had two legs mounted on a platform of tiny wheels. He rolled the legs back and forth on the wooden floor, pleased with the result, then set them aside.

Before starting on the arms, he decided to take a break for some cookies. As he walked through the living room, Curtis came running in from the backyard.

"Mom said you're making a robot!"

Jeffrey rolled his eyes. "Yeah. So?"

"Can I help?"

"No way. This isn't baby stuff, you know."

Curtis glared at him. "I'm not a baby!"

"Then why did you go and tell Mom what I said?"

Curtis didn't answer, and Jeffrey continued triumphantly to the kitchen. After his snack, he went back to his room and began work on the arms.

Suddenly, he realized that he would need a body to attach all this to. He thought for a moment, then ran out to the garage. On a shelf in the corner was an old metal bread box. He got that down and was about to return to his room when he noticed an old electrical cord sticking out from underneath his father's workbench. A bold idea was beginning to form. He took the electrical cord and a spool of copper wire, grabbed a metal punch and snuck back to his room.

He stood the bread box on end, with the door in the back. He then used the punch to put two holes in the bottom, and ran the wire through. Then he fed the wire through the center of each leg and wound it around each foot. As he attached the legs to the box, he realized his metal creation would stand nearly three feet tall!

Next, he drove a metal rod through the sides of the box, near the top. On each end he put a small wheel for the shoulders. Then he attached two short metal rods to each shoulder, and at the opposite end of the rods he screwed on another wheel to act as the elbow.

Jeffrey sat back and chewed on a fingernail while he studied the arms. What was he going to use for hands? Then, with a smile, he scrambled to his feet and shot out to the garage.

He dug through his father's toolbox and managed to come up with two pairs of pliers. He returned to his room and stripped the rubber off of the plier handles. Then he attached a pair to each arm to act as the robot's hands.

For the finishing touch, he went to the kitchen, got a coffee can from the cupboard and emptied the coffee into a bowl. Then he took the can out to the garage and selected two red Christmas lights for the eyes. He also grabbed a regular light bulb to attach to the top of the head.

On his way back to his room, he saw Curtis playing. "Hey, kid," he said, stopping. "You really want to help me with my robot?"

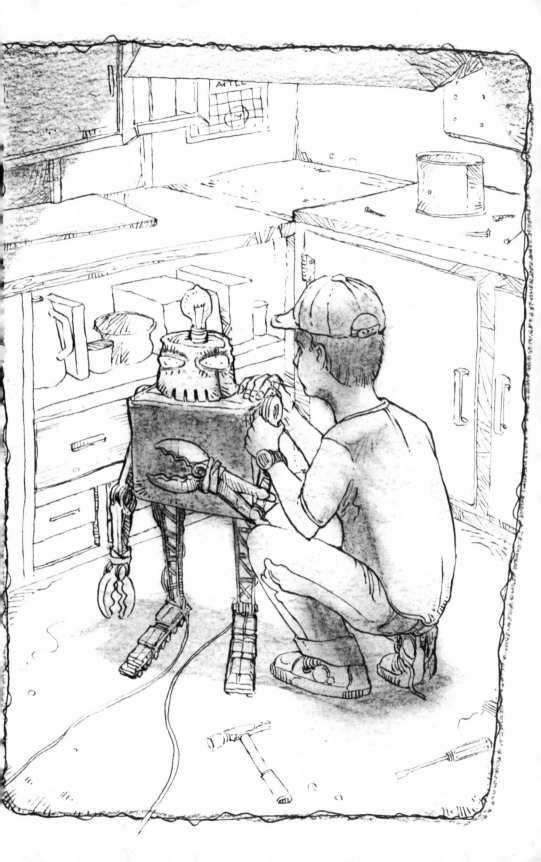

Curtis stood up. "Yeah! What do I have to do?"

"It's easy. Just go to the field and see if you can catch a lizard."

"A lizard?" he said with a suspicious look. "Why?"

Jeffrey shook his head. "Do you want to help or not?"

"All right. But you know Mom won't let me go by myself."

Jeffrey considered this. "Yeah. Okay, let's both go." He went and dumped the coffee can and the lights in his bedroom. Then he and Curtis told their mother where they were going and left.

The field—which was actually a huge, overgrown vacant lot—was a couple of blocks away. All the kids in the neighborhood used it for bike trails, hide-and-seek and any other game they could think of. When Jeffrey and his brother arrived, however, the field was empty.

"Okay," Jeffrey said. "A really big lizard would be best, but I guess any size will work."

"What's it for?" asked Curtis.

In a burst of goodwill, Jeffrey told him. "I'm going to use the lizard to bring my robot to life!"

Curtis was amazed. "How?"

"The lizard will move the robot's arms and legs when it moves its own."

Curtis's eyes lit up. "Wow! Do you really think it'll work?"

"Sure. Why not?" Jeffrey pointed to the far end of the lot. "You take that half and I'll take this one, okay?"

Curtis nodded and took off. Jeffrey began scouting the weeds around him.

After an hour or so, Jeffrey was ready to quit. He had scoured his half of the field, and the only lizard he had seen had managed to escape. He decided to go see how Curtis was doing.

He found his brother crawling through the weeds near the middle of the field.

"Any luck?" he asked.

"Uh-uh. I saw a dead one, but no live ones."

Jeffrey nodded and kicked at a pile of dirt. Then it hit him. A dead lizard! That would be even better!

"Where was that dead lizard?" he demanded.

"Umm. Over there somewhere. Why?"

"Remember that movie *Frankenstein*?"

Curtis nodded. That one had scared him so bad he hadn't slept all night. Jeffrey had talked the babysitter into letting them watch it.

"Remember how Dr. Frankenstein brought the monster to life?" Jeffrey continued. "He put together the parts of dead people and then zapped them with lightning."

"Yeah, so?"

"So. I'll do the same thing with the lizard!"

"What? Wait for lightning?"

"No," said Jeffrey scornfully. "I don't need that much electricity. I'll use a regular outlet."

"I don't know," said Curtis. "Do you think that's a good idea?"

"Don't be such a scaredy-cat! Come on. Where's the lizard?"

Curtis led him to the body. It was about six inches long head to toe and slightly dried out from the sun. Jeffrey found an old milk carton and put his prize inside.

As they got home, Jeffrey turned to his brother. "Now, listen. You had better not tell Mom or Dad about this—or I'll have my robot eat you up!"

"I won't say anything," Curtis muttered.

"Good," said Jeffrey, as he started up the front steps.

He immediately went back to work on his robot. He grabbed the coffee can, stuck it on top of the bread box and punched two holes in the front. He poked the light bulbs through the holes and twisted a loop of copper wire around each one. Then he brought the wire down through the head into the body, and laid the loose end at the bottom of the bread box. Next, he wrapped another piece of wire around the metal rod on which the arms hung, and he let that piece of wire hang to the bottom, also.

He carefully rolled his creation out to the garage. Then it was back to his room to get the lizard, the old electrical cord and some scissors.

On his way back out he collected his brother. "Do you want to see this?" Curtis didn't have to be asked twice and jumped up after his brother.

"Wow," he whispered when he saw the robot. He turned to Jeffrey. "What are you going to do now?"

Jeffrey placed the lizard body into the bottom of the bread box. He connected both of the robot's leg wires to the lizard's hind legs. He took the wire that was looped around the arm rod and wrapped it under the legs on the lizard's upper body. The wire leading to the coffee can was wrapped around the lizard's head.

Then Jeffrey took the scissors and cut off one end of the

electrical cord. He split the two wires apart and cut the insulation from the tip of each one. Then he stuck the two bare wires into the lizard's body. He carefully closed the door of the box, and uncoiled the electric cord.

He stepped back and proudly surveyed his achievement. His robot was ready for life!

Taking the plug of the electric cord to a wall socket, he looked over at his brother. "Ready?" he asked, smiling.

Curtis was too frightened to speak. He just nodded. Jeffrey paused dramatically, then plugged the cord into the socket.

There was a pop from inside the robot, and the eyes lit up. A glow shone from atop the creature's head. Curtis screamed and backed away. Then smoke began pouring out of the back, and a disgusting smell filled the room. Suddenly, the light bulbs dimmed and went out. Jeffrey unplugged the cord.

The smell was getting worse, and Jeffrey had to keep swallowing. Curtis was crying. Jeffrey went over to his robot and opened the door. A cloud of smoke rolled out, and he waved it away. Lying on the floor of the bread box was the burnt body of the lizard.

Jeffrey whirled to face Curtis. "Will you stop crying!" he whispered angrily.

Curtis gulped his way into silence.

"Gosh," Jeffrey said. "What a baby!" Then he stormed out of the garage, leaving his brother behind with the failed experiment.

An hour or so later, Jeffrey figured he had better clean up his mess in the garage. His dad would be home soon, and he didn't want to get in trouble for leaving his stuff all over the place.

But when he walked into the garage, the robot was gone! The electrical cord still snaked across the floor to where the robot had stood, but the robot itself was gone.

Jeffrey panicked for a moment. And then he rolled his eyes and shook his head—his brother had probably hidden it to get even with him. Jeffrey cleaned up what was left, and while he was doing that some of his friends came by. They were going to the lot, and Jeffrey hopped on his bike and joined them.

By that night, he had nearly forgotten about the robot. But after dinner, he followed his brother into his room.

"What did you do with my robot?" he demanded.

Curtis looked at him. "Nothing. Why?"

"C'mon, spud. Where is it?"

Curtis shook his head. "I don't know! Honest."

Jeffrey thought about beating it out of him, but decided that he'd just ignore him instead. Sooner or later, Curtis would confess.

"All right," he said, leaving. "But I'd better not find out you're lying." And, true to his plan, he ignored his brother for the rest of the evening. When his parents came to say good night, he didn't mention the robot.

In the middle of the night, something woke him up. He lay there, staring into the darkness, straining his ears. He heard it again! A tiny, squeaking sound.

He rolled over on his back and pushed himself up. His breath came faster. There was somebody in the house!

The squeaking came closer, and Jeffrey suddenly smiled

in relief. He knew what that sound was. It was the sound of wheels rolling across the floor. That's what Curtis was up to!

The squeaking seemed to be right outside his door. Suddenly, it stopped. Jeffrey slid out of bed and crept over to the door; when his brother came in, he'd scare him to death.

The door slowly swung open. And standing in the doorway was the robot! Jeffrey jumped in front of it and growled.

The robot's eyes glowed faintly red, and the bulb on the top of its head flickered weakly. It stood still with its arms extended. Curtis was nowhere in sight.

"Curtis?" he whispered. Then the robot shot forward and drove its arms into his throat.

The Girl of Their Dreams

isa stood at her bedroom window and watched the moving van pull away from the old Muller place. The house stood in the middle of a huge piece of vacant land on the edge of town, and Lisa's house was on a street that ran along one side of the lot. Her bedroom window stared straight at the huge, decaying mansion. It had been empty for as long as she could remember. But this evening, just before sunset, a van had pulled up in front of the house. Two men had unloaded a couple of large boxes from the back and driven off.

"Have you seen anybody yet?" asked Chris, her brother, from behind her.

"No. Just the two moving guys. I wonder who would buy such an ugly old place?"

Chris shrugged. "Ugly old people?" he suggested. Lisa snickered, and followed him down to the dinner table.

That night, she dreamed that a beautiful princess had moved into the Muller house, and she wanted Lisa to come and stay with her. So Lisa moved into the house, and there she found everything she had ever wanted, all waiting for her.

Lisa woke in the middle of the night feeling strange. She felt jumpy and cranky, like she was hungry. The dream was still clear in her mind, however, and she slipped out of bed and went to her window.

The windows of the abandoned house were dark. But its ancient walls seemed to shimmer in the moonlight, as if they were magically clean and white again. She stared at it for a while, then shook her head and went back to bed.

The next morning, Chris surprised her by asking if she wanted to come check out the new people at the Muller house. Still thinking about her dream, Lisa agreed quickly.

They got dressed, then picked their way across the field. As they got closer to the house, Lisa could see that the broken windows had been boarded up. The remaining ones had heavy blinds drawn in front of them.

They came around to the front of the house, and Chris stepped onto the porch.

"Wait, Chris!" Lisa whispered loudly. "What if someone's home?"

"Well why else are we here?" he snapped. "If you're too afraid, go home!"

She thought about it, but then she remembered her dream. There was no way she was going to miss out on this one. "Go ahead and knock," she said.

Chris stepped forward and rapped on the heavy wooden door. After a moment, the front door creaked open, and a man stood there. He smiled when he saw Lisa and her brother. "Hello. Can I help you?"

"Uh, hi," Chris began. "I'm Chris Kohler and this is my sister, Lisa. We live in the blue house across the field. We saw you move in yesterday and came over to meet you."

The man nodded, still smiling. "My name is Benjamin. My daughter, Brinn, and I just bought this house."

"You have a daughter?" Lisa asked abruptly.

"Yes. But she hasn't arrived yet. Maybe you could come by this evening after dinner? I'm sure she'd like to meet you."

"Sure," Lisa said.

"Okay," agreed Chris. "See you later."

As they walked back home, Chris asked Lisa, "Why were you so surprised he has a daughter?"

"I—I had a dream about the house."

Chris spun around and stared at her. "What do you mean?"

She stopped, surprised by his reaction. "I dreamed that a princess lived there. And that she was very lonely and wanted me to come live with her. And she gave me diamonds and jewelry and all sorts of things."

Chris stared at her. "Me, too! I mean, I had a dream about the Muller house, too."

Lisa's mouth dropped open. "Yeah? Was there a

99

princess?"

Chris shook his head. "No. I dreamed it was more like a museum, with all sorts of old swords and armor and stuff!"

Lisa didn't know what to think. She and Chris had always been very close, but they had never shared the same dreams. "This is weird, Chris."

He nodded in agreement, and they returned to their house.

That night, after dinner, they told their mother they were going to visit the new girl at the Muller house. Back across the field they went, this time under the pale glow of dusk.

The door was opened as soon as they stepped onto the porch. A girl stood in the doorway, outlined by the wash of light from inside. She was very pretty, with long black hair and dark eyes. She smiled at them. "Hello. My name is Brinn."

Lisa felt as if she had found an old friend. She shot a glance at her brother. He was staring at Brinn with his mouth slightly open like a dead fish. She poked him with her elbow as she stepped slightly forward. "I'm Lisa," she announced. "And this is my brother, Chris. We live in the blue house across the field."

Brinn nodded. "Come in." She stepped back to allow Lisa and her brother inside. The interior was lit by what seemed like hundreds of candles in gleaming brass candelabra. To one side of the living room was a polished wooden staircase rising up to a darkened second floor. "The electricity's not on yet," Brinn explained. "My father's gone into town to see if he can find an open hardware store." Brinn led them to a big, overstuffed sofa and motioned for

them to have a seat.

"I'm really glad you two came over," said Brinn as they sat down. "I always like to meet new people. Is this a nice neighborhood?"

"It's okay," answered Chris. He proceeded to tell Brinn about some of the other kids who lived nearby.

"So," Lisa asked Brinn when he finished, "where do you and your dad come from?"

"We move around a lot." Brinn shrugged and laughed. "I don't even remember where I was born anymore!"

"Have you ever been to another country?" asked Chris.

"Oh, yes. We used to live in Europe."

"Really?" asked Lisa, sitting forward. "Where?"

Brinn began telling them of all the different places she could remember visiting while she lived in Europe. Chris and Lisa listened in fascination.

Suddenly, Lisa looked at her watch. They had been sitting here for more than two hours! It was almost nine o'clock. "Come on, Chris," she said, getting to her feet. "We have to get home."

Brinn rose with them. "I'm glad we got to know each other. Thank you for coming over."

Chris nodded. "Want to come over to our house tomorrow?"

Brinn shook her head. "I can't. I was very sick for a while, and my father wants me to stay inside and get as much rest as possible."

"You're okay now, aren't you?" asked Lisa with concern.

"Oh, yes. Not one hundred percent, but better." She smiled shyly. "It really helps to have someone to talk to."

"We can come back here tomorrow," Chris offered. Lisa nodded in agreement.

"That would be great," Brinn said. "Why not come over tomorrow evening?"

So the next night they returned to Brinn's house. Lisa didn't talk to Chris about it, but she could tell that he liked Brinn as much as she did. The girl was fairly quiet, but she always had some interesting story to tell. Soon, it became a nightly ritual to go over to Brinn's house and sit in the living room, talking. They rarely saw Brinn's father, but he didn't seem to mind the constant company for his daughter.

One night, after Lisa and Chris had returned home and gone to bed, Lisa had a horrible dream. She dreamed that Brinn was dying, and she was the only person who could help her. But for some reason, she was not able to. She watched helplessly as Brinn sat in the middle of her living room and slowly withered away.

Lisa woke up sweating. Then, on a hunch, she snuck down the hall to her brother's room and opened the door. "Chris," she whispered. "It's me."

"What?"

"I just had a nightmare about Brinn."

Chris looked at her strangely. "What was it about?" he asked.

"I dreamed that she was dying and I had the power to save her. But I couldn't get to her."

Chris was silent for a long moment. Then he said, "I had a dream like that, too. What do you think it means?"

Lisa thought for a moment. "Maybe she's more sick than she told us. And we're both picking that up somehow."

"That could be. Let's ask her tomorrow, okay?"

Lisa agreed and went back to her room. The rest of the night she slept without dreaming.

The next day, as soon as they were up, they got dressed and ran over to Brinn's house. They knocked and rang the bell, but nobody answered. Lisa tried to peer into the windows, but all the shades were pulled down.

The rest of that day, one or the other of them made sure to keep an eye on the house. But they never saw Brinn or her father. That night, after dinner, they tried again.

This time Brinn opened the front door. Lisa jumped slightly. "Brinn! We didn't see you come home!"

Brinn smiled. "I haven't gone anywhere."

"But we came by earlier," said Chris. "And nobody answered."

Brinn shrugged. "I must have been asleep." She opened the door wider. "But come in. I've finally managed to unpack everything, and I'd like to show you something."

Brinn led them through the front room, where her father sat reading. He didn't look up as they walked by him and down a brightly painted hallway. "I think you'll like this room," she said to Chris, opening a door. Chris looked inside and couldn't believe his eyes. The room was filled with swords and weapons of every style. Shields hung on the wall with faded banners. Suits of armor lined the sides of the room like soldiers at attention.

"Wow!" he practically yelled as he darted forward into the room. Lisa pressed forward to see, but Brinn stepped in front of her.

"What was he so excited about?" she asked, puzzled. All

she had seen was some rusty old plumbing sticking out of the wall.

"You know how boys are," Brinn answered, leading Lisa to another room.

Before Lisa could ask her what she meant, Brinn had opened the door to the next room. Now it was Lisa's turn to gasp in wonder. The room was lined with display cases. Each one had piles of jewels and necklaces and rings and everything else Lisa could imagine. It was just like her dream! She stepped forward, hardly knowing where to start looking.

"I'll be right back," Brinn said. She closed the door behind her, leaving Lisa in the room alone.

Lisa lost herself in examining the wealth around her. She moved slowly from case to case, mesmerized by the treasures displayed.

After a while, she thought of Chris. She straightened and looked around the room in confusion. She had a strong feeling that something was wrong. "Chris?" she asked in a soft voice. Then she ran for the door. "Chris!"

She flung the door open and froze. The hallway was dark and smelled of damp plaster. The shining candelabra were gone, and in their place were single candles set on the floor. The painted walls were actually covered with peeling wallpaper faded with age.

Lisa took a deep breath and plunged down the hallway to the room where she had left her brother. The door was hanging on one hinge, and when she pushed it open it tore itself out of the frame with a screech and crashed to the floor. Lisa jumped back in fear, too startled to speak.

The room was empty. The walls in here had nearly collapsed, and bits of plumbing were revealed like the bones of a corpse. For some reason, there were pie tins nailed to the walls, with old pieces of rags hanging next to them.

"Chris!" Lisa yelled. "Chris! Where are you?" Then her mouth snapped shut, as she heard a loud crash upstairs.

"Lisa!" her brother screamed from somewhere above her. "Get out!"

Heart pounding, breath coming in short gasps, Lisa ran from the room. She turned down the hallway toward the living room. The scenery had changed here as well. The fine, rich furniture was just old boxes of trash! She wanted her brother! What was happening to him? "Chris!" she screamed as her eyes darted around the room.

Then she saw it. The true form of the sofa. It was a coffin, set in the middle of the room like a prized possession. Curled up on one end of it was a withered skeleton wearing the clothes that Brinn's father had been wearing. Lisa stared at the clothes, trying to accept what her mind was telling her. To her horror the coffin lid began to rise. As she edged toward the door, a whiskered snout pushed its way out from under the lid. This was followed by the biggest rat she had ever imagined. It perched on the edge of the coffin and stared at her.

She saw movement out of the corner of her eye and whipped her head around to look at the staircase. Her brother staggered into view. "Chris!" she screamed.

He turned toward her and her heart seemed to stop. The left side of his shirt was covered with blood. It seemed to spray from a wound in his throat. He saw his sister and pointed to the door. "Run!" he said in a hoarse voice.

Then Brinn pounced into view. She was taller and older now, about the age of their mother. Her mouth was smeared with blood, and she advanced on Chris with hunger in her eyes.

Lisa's legs buckled, and her vision swam in and out of focus. Another scream from her brother jerked her head up. Brinn was standing over him, mouth fastened on his neck.

"No," Lisa whispered. Then, louder, "No!" She scrambled to her feet and bolted for the door. She wrenched it open and practically flew off the porch and into the field. Sobbing and choking, she somehow made it across the field to her house. She fumbled at the doorknob, then thrust herself inside.

She stopped in complete confusion. She was back inside the Muller house! The door creaked shut behind her, and she slowly turned to look.

Brinn stood there, smiling with red teeth. Her fangs gleamed in the light of the candles as she bent forward and clutched Lisa to her.

A Wolf in Sheep's Clothing

id you hear about last night?" Jerry asked Craig as he rushed into class before the bell.

"Uh-uh, was there another one?" asked Craig.

"Yeah!" said Linda from the seat in front of them. "A delivery guy. They found him in an alley!"

"The *whole* alley," added Robert with great emphasis.

"What do you mean?" asked Craig, as the bell rang and kids started scrambling for their seats.

"Well," said Robert, "they found an arm at one end of the alley, and by the time they walked to the other end they had managed to find most of the rest of his body—"

"Robert!" The voice of Mr. Pender, the teacher, cut

through the class. Robert swung guiltily around in his chair.

"Sorry," he said.

Mr. Pender slowly looked around the class. "All right," he said. "I suppose most of you have heard that there's been another killing."

An excited buzz filled the classroom. Throughout the fall, the police had been finding the bodies of people brutally murdered. So far, eight victims had been found. Most of the time their bodies were slashed up so badly that they were in pieces. The story was on the news almost every night, as the police tried to find out who the killer could be.

"That's what I thought," continued Mr. Pender. "Well, it's because of these deaths that I've invited a special guest here today."

For a brief moment, Craig had a vision of a wild-eyed killer springing into the room with a meat cleaver. Instead, the door was opened by a young policeman.

"I've asked Officer McCann here today to talk to all of you about safety. So please give him your attention." Mr. Pender turned to the policeman and gestured for him to start.

"Hi, class," said Officer McCann.

"Hi!" they all yelled back.

"I want to talk to you all today about safety," began the policeman. "Now I know you've probably heard lectures from your parents already, but we at the police department want everybody to keep their eyes open and be just a little more careful than usual."

"Officer McCann," said Teresa in a loud voice. "Do you have any clues about the Autumn Slasher?"

"Well, I'm sure you understand that I can't reveal any details about the investigation. I can tell you, though, that we do have some clues to go on, and we're doing our best to put them together and catch this criminal."

He walked over and hitched one leg up on the corner of Mr. Pender's desk. "But while the case is still open, it's very important for all of us to be as careful as we can. Now, how many of you can tell me what you should do if you're approached by a stranger?"

Craig tuned out as the policeman lectured the class on safety. He knew all of that stuff; he had heard it from his father. He looked around at his classmates. Most of them were listening to the policeman. Some, like Jack, the new kid, seemed to be daydreaming. Jack was staring out the window, and Craig wondered what he was thinking about. Soon, Craig was lost in a daydream too.

At recess, the newest murder was the big topic of conversation.

"My dad says the police don't have any idea who's behind it," pronounced Bruce.

"But Officer McCann said they had some clues," Teresa protested.

"I think it's some kind of monster," said Jack. "I mean, who knows what kind of weird things live in the sewers and in abandoned houses?"

"You really think so?" asked Gina with wide eyes.

"Why not?" said Jack, his voice dropping lower. "Maybe late at night, after we're all asleep, some hideous, flesh-eating creature climbs out of the drains and goes hunting for dinner."

"That's ridiculous," scoffed Craig.

"Oh yeah?" asked Jack. "Do you have a better idea?"

"It's probably just some kind of psycho," answered Craig.

"I agree," said Teresa. "My parents are always telling me to stay away from strangers. I've heard it at least once a day since the killing began."

"Yeah. Why invent some kind of stupid monster?" asked Brian. "The best thing you can do is just stay away from strangers, like Teresa said."

Most of the other kids nodded. "And don't go out alone," Craig added.

"Well, my dad says there are plenty of things we don't know about," answered Jack angrily.

"That's right," said Anthony, jumping into the conversation. "What about all those scientific studies on ghosts and stuff like that?"

This prompted an all-out argument about monsters and ghosts and other weird things. By the time the bell interrupted their discussion nothing was clear except that Craig and Jack each thought the other one was a jerk.

The second half of the day passed by uneventfully. About halfway through class, Craig noticed Jack glaring at him, but he ignored him. He couldn't help it if Jack was mad at him. It was nothing personal. It was his fault for having such dumb ideas about monsters and stuff.

When the final bell rang, the kids gathered up their books and poured out into the yard. Craig joined some of the other boys in a football game and forgot all about psycho killers for a while.

He didn't leave the school until late in the afternoon. Most of the other kids had already been picked up by their parents. Some, like Anthony, were hanging around the front of the school, waiting. As Craig walked out of the yard, Anthony called to him, "You'd better hope there's no such thing as monsters!"

Craig ignored him. He didn't care if Anthony wanted to believe those stupid stories about ghosts and monsters. He didn't know everything, but he knew there was no such thing as flesh-eating monsters that lived in the sewers!

He jerked his book bag over one shoulder. Kids like Anthony were just jealous of him because *his* parents didn't treat him like a kid. He was allowed to walk home from school; he didn't have to wait for his parents to pick him up like the other kids.

He sighed. He also had to admit to himself that there was really no reason for anybody to be jealous of him. The only reason his parents allowed him to walk home was because they were too busy to come pick him up after school. His dad was a lawyer and almost always had to stay late at the office. His mom ran a clothing store, and her favorite complaint was that something was "always coming up at the last minute."

So they told Craig that he had to "act like an adult." That was his dad's favorite phrase. That's why he was positive there were no such things as monsters. Adults didn't believe in that kind of stuff.

But sometimes acting like an adult was hard to do. Especially when that meant walking home from school alone, when there was some maniac prowling around waiting to stick a knife into the nearest person.

At the thought, he snuck a quick glance over his left shoulder. The street was empty. He snorted and turned forward.

He really had stayed at school longer than he should have. Now he was about halfway home and nighttime was creeping in. The truth was, he had forgotten that it was getting dark a little bit earlier every day.

One by one, the street lights flickered and burned on. He was walking down a long street lined by closed shops and black windows. He was trying not to think about the darkening sky when he heard something behind him. Trying not to look scared, he casually glanced over his shoulder. His breath caught in his throat. *What was that?* He stopped and stared down the street behind him. Nothing moved. But hadn't he just seen a shadowy figure duck into the doorway of one of the shops?

His heart kicked into high gear. He turned around and started walking faster. In the back of his mind, he thought that he still had to act casual; he had to act like nothing was wrong. That way, somehow, nothing *would* be wrong. Like his dad always said, "Act like a victim, and you'll be a victim." He straightened his shoulders and held his head up.

He darted another look behind him. He saw nothing. *But he could feel someone watching him!* He walked a little faster, his breath whistling in and out between his teeth. His eyes anxiously scanned both sides of the street. He searched up ahead of him for an open shop, a welcome glimmer of light that meant there was a phone inside to use. A place where he wouldn't have to act like an adult.

Then he heard it. The soft scrape of a footstep behind him. He whirled around! But the street was still deserted. His heart began pounding painfully. He forgot about acting like a victim and broke into a run.

His book bag thudded against his shoulder as he raced down the street. Why did everything in this stupid town close so early! There was not another person in sight. Now he was sure he could hear footsteps behind him. This time he was too afraid to look back. He tried to run faster.

Suddenly, a side street appeared. Without thinking, he ducked around the corner and ran into someone! He screamed as he and the stranger both stumbled and fell.

"Jeez! What are you trying to do, kill me?" a familiar voice angrily shouted.

Craig looked up in disbelief. Picking himself off the ground was Jack.

"What's the matter with you?" Jack demanded.

"I think he's after me!" Craig gulped in air.

"Who?"

"The killer. I think he's behind me!"

Jack looked around in fear. "Oh man! Are you sure?"

Craig nodded.

"Okay, okay," he muttered, looking left to right. "We'd better get out of here. Come on, let's go this way."

Craig scrambled to his feet and ran after Jack. It was obvious that Jack knew the area, because he led them down a couple of side streets and then an alley without stopping to look. Craig kept looking behind them, but nobody appeared.

MISSING

Suddenly, he realized that they were in a dead end. Jack had stopped. He looked like he was staring at the wall in front of them. Was he looking for some secret passageway? Was he going to climb it?

"What are you doing?" Craig asked Jack from behind. "How will we get out of here?"

Jack made a noise that sounded like a cross between laughing and coughing. "We won't," he answered.

"What do you mean?"

Jack turned around. Thick, brown hair was sprouting from his face. His body seemed to bulge out in strange places under his clothes. He held up a hand with razor-sharp claws.

"So," he rasped. "You still don't believe in monsters?"

The Thrill-Seekers' Club

"All right," announced Peter. "I'll do it." He stared defiantly at the other boys in the tree house. More than anything, Peter wanted to be a part of the Thrill-Seekers' Club. Everybody did—it was *the* club to be in. All of the other boys in the Thrill-Seekers were older than Peter, but he was sure he could prove to them that he was brave enough to be in their club.

"Okay," said Andy, who was eleven years old and the leader. "We'll meet back here tomorrow morning. If you have the flowerpot from Old Man Stamper's grave, then you're in the club." The other boys nodded in agreement.

"And if you're not here," added Matt, "then we'll know

you were too afraid to do it."

"Either that," said Andy, "or Old Man Stamper got you!"

The older boys laughed as they climbed one by one down the wooden ladder nailed against the tree that held the clubhouse. Peter waited a moment, then he climbed down too and trudged back to the street.

He stopped in the field at the edge of the forest. From where he stood, he could see the late afternoon sun shining on the giant iron gate of the Final Haven Cemetery. It was the town's only graveyard, and it had been there forever. The town's first mayor was buried there, and he had died nearly a hundred years ago.

Mr. Finch, the cemetery gardener, seemed like he'd been around for the last hundred years too. He was a strange man who lived in a small cottage near the very center of the cemetery. He almost never came outside the walls of the cemetery, except to close the gate every night.

Peter had seen Mr. Finch only once. He was tall and thin, had completely white hair, and he hitched one leg up when he walked. A slightly hunched back made him look kind of spooky, and he always wore a black shirt and black pants. On cold days he wore a heavy black overcoat.

Peter was starting to have second thoughts. If Finch caught him, his dad was sure to find out. And he knew he'd be grounded for the rest of his life if that happened! He tried to convince himself he wasn't scared as he passed the cemetery and headed home.

When he got there, his best friend David was sitting on the front porch, waiting for him. "Well?" asked David as Peter walked up. "What happened? Are they going to let you in?"

Peter put his finger to his lips and crept around to the side of the house. David followed. "I think so," Peter answered. "But first the guys want me to prove I'm not chicken."

"How are you gonna do that?"

"I have to go to the cemetery tonight and steal the flowerpot from Old Man Stamper's grave."

David's eyes grew wide. "Tonight? When it's pitch black? In the cemetery? What are you, crazy?"

Peter hushed him angrily. This was not what he wanted to hear. "Big deal," he said. "It's just a dumb flowerpot. And I've been through the cemetery before."

"Yeah, but never at night," David replied. "And besides, how are you going to get out of the house without your parents knowing?"

"I'm going to wait until they go to sleep. Then I'll sneak out the back door."

David threw his hands in the air. "Oh, man. That means you won't get to the cemetery until almost midnight!"

Peter didn't answer. David poked at a spider with his toe. After a long silence he spoke.

"Well," said David. "I can't understand why you want to get into that stupid club. But since you do," he took a deep breath, "I'll go with you tonight if you want."

Peter felt a wave of relief. "Great! I'll come by tonight and knock on your window! Around eleven!"

After dinner, Peter watched television with his dad for a while, then went to bed. He lay there in silent anticipation until he heard his parents go to bed. Then he quietly, carefully got dressed and crept to the back door. He opened it slowly and squeezed outside.

It was a cool night, and he ran nearly all the way to David's house. When he got there, he rapped softly on his friend's bedroom window. Within seconds, David's face appeared. He gave Peter the thumbs-up sign and was outside a minute later.

"I can't believe we're doing this!" David said as they made their way up the street, trying to stay in the shadows.

By the time they reached the cemetery, clouds had begun to cover the moon. There was just enough light from the street lamps to see the gate, but Peter knew it would be dark inside. Why hadn't he remembered to bring a flashlight?

"How are we going to get in?" David asked.

Peter surveyed the huge gate. The bars were too close together to squeeze through. "We'll have to climb over," he decided. And without waiting for David's answer, he climbed over the gate. David followed right behind him.

Once on the other side, they paused to stare down the long central path of the cemetery. Twisted oaks clung to the edge of the path, forming a dark tunnel. More trees dotted the graveyard landscape, lurking in the black pools of their shadows. Peter thought he heard something moving in the branches, but he couldn't see any birds or breeze.

The remaining space around them was filled with monuments to the dead. To either side of the dirt path, gravestones, statues and crosses seemed to grow out of the ground. Whenever the moon would float from behind the clouds, the mix of white stones and crazily angled shadows was almost too confusing to look at.

"I still think this is crazy," David whispered. "Are you sure you want to do this? Let's forget about it. We can form our own club!"

Peter was really tempted to agree. But he took a deep breath and shook his head. He had come this far, he might as well go through with it. "Come on," he said, moving cautiously forward. "Andy told me that Stamper's grave is toward the back of the cemetery, in the oldest part."

"Oh, great," David hissed. But he followed his friend.

The farther they got from the gate, the darker their surroundings became. The oak trees seemed to strain toward them as they bravely made their way forward. The clouds had almost completely covered the moon by now, and except for the sound of their own footsteps, the cemetery was eerily quiet. Even the birds had stopped moving.

Finally, they reached the end of the path, where a small chapel hunched under the trees.

"Can we go back now?" David asked.

Peter stopped abruptly and swung to face his friend. "Look, are you with me or not?" he whispered loudly. "All we have to do is get the flowerpot and go!"

"Okay, okay," David replied. "Let's get it over with."

Peter nodded. "Come on. It's not much farther."

They quickly passed by the chapel and began picking their way through the tombstones. Once in a while the moon would shine through a hole in the clouds, helping them to see. Here in the old part of the cemetery, the trees were very big. They seemed to be closer, too, as if wanting to grab the two boys. The grass was thick and uncut, and

ivy covered many of the tombstones. Crooked stones and broken statues were everywhere.

Suddenly, Peter looked up and they were there! A huge tombstone stood before them, and at the top of the stone Peter read the name: STAMPER. Off to one side was a small clay flowerpot with some dried flowers in it.

Peter lunged for the pot, but it was stuck in the ground and wouldn't pull free! No matter how hard he tried, he could not get it to move. In anger, he kicked at the pot but missed and hit the tombstone instead.

"Will you hurry up!" hissed David as Peter hopped from foot to foot.

"The stupid thing is stuck!"

David came over and the two boys tugged on the pot. Suddenly, there was a crash as the thing shattered in their hands. They stared at the pot for a moment. Then there was a grunting sound from the trees to their right. The two boys looked at each other in terror. With a sob, David bolted for the front of the cemetery.

"Wait!" Peter cried out, but his voice didn't seem to work. He grabbed a piece of the flowerpot and took off through the tombstones after David. But as he heard the snapping of branches behind him his legs seemed to stop working. He stumbled over something and tumbled headfirst to the ground. Panting in fear, he scrambled to get his feet under him.

Just then, a hand grabbed his shoulder. Peter spun around, his heart beating so fast it felt like it would explode.

It was Mr. Finch. Peter couldn't see his face, but he was dressed in black, as usual. Except instead of his black overcoat he was wearing something like a robe with a hood. Mr. Finch did not speak, but yanked Peter to his feet and began pulling him forward.

Peter let himself be led. He knew he should be worried about what his parents would say when Mr. Finch told them he'd been caught sneaking around the cemetery at night, but he was still trying to recover his breath. And David! That chicken! He was going to get out of it! Peter sighed. At least he'd be able to prove to the Thrill-Seekers' Club that he had been here.

The moon came out from behind a cloud and, in the pale light, Peter could see that they were walking deeper into the cemetery.

"Hey, Mr. Finch," he said. "This isn't the way to the front gate." They stopped.

"No," came the answer as the figure turned toward him. Peter screamed in horror as he saw the rotting, skeletal face of the thing that held him. But as the creature pulled him closer, he realized that only the dead could hear him.